WELCOME TO WYOMING

The sheriff stepped back. "Your pa, he was pretty big stuff, but he got took down to size. You and these two hirelings of yours mess around here, you'll get took down to size the same way."

Ki's hand streaked out, and he slapped the lawman across the mouth. "Don't ever threaten her life again," he whispered.

The man roared and jumped at Ki, and the samurai sent a flat-foot kick straight into that big belly. The sheriff groaned. His cheeks puffed out and he staggered. Ki moved in and kicked him in the buttocks and he went crashing into the jail cell . . .

The sheriff clawed for his gun, but Jessie had anticipated that and she had her own gun out and pointed at his head. "Don't do it, Sheriff."

"Miss Starbuck, you may be a big deal in Texas, but this is Wyoming and you're nothing! You'll be sorry you ever came to Skull Creek. Both of you!"

•◆• WESLEY ELLIS •◆•

LONE STAR

IN A RANGE WAR

J
JOVE BOOKS, NEW YORK

LONE STAR IN A RANGE WAR

A Jove Book / published by arrangement with
the author

PRINTING HISTORY
Jove edition / October 1987

ISBN: 0-515-09216-9

Jove Books are published by The Berkley Publishing Group,
200 Madison Avenue, New York, New York 10016.
The name "JOVE" and the "J" logo
are trademarks belonging to Jove Publications, Inc.

PRINTED IN THE UNITED STATES OF AMERICA

10 9 8 7 6 5 4 3 2 1

Chapter 1

Jessica Starbuck rode a horse as if she had been born in the saddle. She and Sun, her beautiful palomino stallion, made a striking pair, for both were sleek and graceful, golden colored and high spirited. But right now, they were playing a very, very dangerous game with a wild longhorn whose horns probably spanned six feet and were as deadly as rapiers.

It was roundup time on the vast Circle Star ranch, which covered thousands of acres down in Southwest Texas. The spring sky was cloudless. Jessie was a woman who could dress like a cowgirl and look splendid, or be absolutely stunning in an evening gown. She adapted to any and all circumstances, a trait that she guessed she'd inherited from her father, Alex Starbuck. Murdered years ago by a sinister European cartel interested in gaining control of America's burgeoning industries, Alex had left his stamp on Circle Star. Jessie could not ride an hour across this wild and beautiful range without remembering something he had taught her, had said that she needed to remember during good times and bad.

Whenever Jessie thought about her late father, she felt a

flush of pride that he had risen from obscurity to become one of the world's wealthiest men. Alex Starbuck had begun to build his fortune after opening a small shop in San Francisco, where he'd dealt in jade and ivory treasures from the Far East. He had quickly expanded into international shipping and then branched into steel, diamonds, railroads, and a fleet of revolutionary iron-hulled merchant vessels that he built in his own bustling shipyards. There was nothing that Alex Starbuck touched that did not succeed. Today, under Jessica's direction and leadership, his far-flung industrial empire still spanned the globe and touched the lives of people in both hemispheres. Maybe, Jessie thought sadly, that was why the cartel had been so relentlessly committed to his murder and why she and her samurai, Ki, had not rested until it had been stamped to death like a deadly rattlesnake.

"Miss Starbuck," her foreman, Ed Wright, called anxiously. "I *sure* wish you'd come out here in the open and let one of your cowboys do that kind of work. You got the best; that's what they're paid to do."

Jessie knew that Ed was worried. She was riding alone through heavy chaparral looking for the dangerous bulls that hid in this brushy maze until cornered. Jessie held a braided leather reata more than forty feet long. She had learned how to rope from the vaqueros, who were the acknowledged masters of the art.

"I'll second that," Ki said from somewhere off to her left. It was clear that her friend the Japanese samurai warrior was also nervous.

Jessie smiled tightly at her samurai's words. She was aware of her own danger. Jessie could barely see the two men because of the thickness and height of the brush. Sometimes she could catch a flash of color moving through the brush, but no more than that. In any event, Jessie's attention was too fixed on what lay ahead to allow any distractions.

She was following a narrow, winding trail which took her and Sun even deeper into this vast sea of Texas chaparral—an impenetrable sea that stretched for miles over much of this hard country and afforded a haven for the wild bulls that raided her herds. Domestic bulls were gored to death and her cows were abducted by these wild beasts of the brush. They had to be stopped.

They were killer animals, faster than deer, more deadly and combative than wild pigs. But they had to be roped, dragged from their strongholds, then unceremoniously branded and castrated. Without their ponderous testicles, and with a brand on their flanks, the mighty killers became as gentle as kittens. In fact, because of their great size and courage, they were often used as the leaders of the trail herds that Jessie's cowboys were gathering to drive north to the railhead towns of Abilene and Leavenworth, Kansas.

"Jessie," Ki complained. "I can't get through this brush if I should need to help you! You should not risk so much."

"But he is just ahead," she said softly. "And I think this is the one that has stolen so many of my good cows during the past winter."

"And the one who gored Pedro Sanchez last fall when he tried to drop a rope over his great horns."

"I know," Jessie conceded. "But Pedro got careless. He admitted it was so. And besides, I have my gun."

Ki said something she could not hear clearly. Jessie smiled, knowing the Japanese samurai had grumbled softly in his own language. It was unusual for the highly disciplined samurai to vent anger or frustration. He was the most unflappable man Jessie had ever known—as well as

3

the deadliest. Ki had no fear of dying, only of failing to protect her life, which he had sworn to protect with his own. And now, she was taking a needless risk. A cowboy could do this job, perhaps even better than she. But what if he got hurt or killed? Could she ever forgive herself for letting another suffer or die because of her lack of resolve? Of course not! All his life, Alex Starbuck had lived without fear and taken chances when he'd needed to. Jessie knew she could do no less.

Jessie heard a small sound just up ahead, and knew that it would be the wild longhorn. The thicket was so tall now that it canopied overhead and shut out the sun. The tunnel of brush she followed seemed to narrow until its thorny branches raked at the thick leather of her boots and covered stirrups.

"Jessie, why—"

"Sssshh!" she whispered. "I think he's just around the next corner."

Her stallion began to tremble. Sun was a brave animal, but here, in the tight confines of this narrow tunnel, neither his speed nor even his quickness would be of any value if the longhorn suddenly charged them. Jessie's eyes dropped to the carbine. Its scarred wooden stock poked out from under her knee. She knew the smart thing to do would be to pull her rifle up and be prepared to kill the animal.

But that would be a waste of a fine animal. The bull deserved a chance to be roped and spared. Had she wanted such animals shot on sight, she would have ordered it to be done. But the cowboys and vaqueros on Circle Star would not have respected her for giving such an order. Anyone could shoot a wild longhorn; it took great skill and courage to go into its lair of brush and bring it out alive to be cut and branded.

4

Sun stopped dead in his tracks. Jessie felt the animal balk for just an instant. She raised her reata, the sound and thick scent of the longhorn filling her nostrils. She could hear her own heartbeat as well as feel that of the stallion's between her legs. Flies buzzed in the still air. Somewhere just ahead, a cow bawled softly and something scuttled away through the brush.

Jessie gently nudged Sun forward with her spurs.

The stallion responded, though it was clearly nervous. Every muscle fiber in her body, every bit of concentration Jessie possessed became focused on the tunnel just ahead where it took a sharp bend. Jessie felt a trickle of sweat river down her backbone.

Come on, she thought, exhaling a deep breath that she had not realized she'd been holding. *Let's get this over with.*

Suddenly, Jessie felt the stallion's lean body tense. Her rope began to whirl overhead an instant before a huge brindle longhorn exploded into view. Jessie had two seconds to either wheel her horse and run in the face of its charge, or throw her reata. She did the latter.

Her forearm snapped forward in very much the same throwing motion that she would use to hurl a Bowie knife. The reata shot forward as if propelled from the mouth of a cannon. By the time it grabbed on to the big span of horn, it was no more than an inch wider than necessary, which was exactly as Jessie had been taught. Anyone could throw a barn-door–sized loop and snag something, but it took an artist to toss a small noose that would grab the bull by the horns like a fist would the throat of an enemy.

Jessie yanked slack. Almost tasting the bull's grassy breath, she whirled her horse and used her spurs. Sun needed no urging as he bolted into a planned retreat. Jessie looked back over her shoulder. In its great fury, the animal would chase her and her stallion out of its safe domain into an open place. There, she would rein the stallion about and try to keep away from its horns long enough for help to arrive. Someone would burst into view, rope the heels of this huge bull, and bust it to the earth. In moments, they would have its back and forelegs tied. While the bull thrashed and ripped the earth with its great horns, they would start a small brush fire. Fifteen minutes later a branding iron would glow cherry red. When it touched the hide of the animal, the hair would send up dense stinking smoke and the bull would go beserk with helpless anger. And a moment later, its half-ton body of muscle, bone and blistered hide would be stretched out even farther and it would be castrated.

Jessie would not stay for the castration. She knew it was necessary to tame the animal, to make it a thing of value to Circle Star rather than an expensive and dangerous liability. But there was something about seeing a male animal castrated that turned her stomach, maybe because she so much appreciated the beauty and the necessity of the act of physical union between the sexes.

"Come on!" she cried to her stallion as it bolted back down the tunnel of brush.

Jessie glanced back to see the bull closing on her. Try as it might, her stallion was at a great disadvantage because of the poor footing and the thin, crumbling trail that these cattle followed into hiding.

It overtook them when Sun had to slow to round a sharp curve. Jessie felt the bull's hot breath, and then felt its horn as it caught her stallion in the flank.

Sun was momentarily knocked off balance. He screamed in pain and Jessie felt his hindquarters cave in.

She reached for her sixgun, and when she twisted around in her saddle, she fired point-blank at the longhorn. Her slug just whanged ineffectually off the animal's thick skull.

Again, the horns of the bull hooked up and into her horse. This time, Sun staggered for an instant as he tried valiantly to whirl and fight with his teeth.

They went crashing down into a small, rocky clearing, and at the very last instant, Jessie kicked free of her stirrups and tried to relax as her body smashed into the hard earth. The impact knocked the wind from her lungs, and her head slammed against the earth. She rolled, feeling the bull charging forward to drive its great horns through her body. Sun screamed in pain and scrambled to his feet. The bull hit the end of her reata, and both animals were jerked off balance and went thrashing to earth. Jessie had lost her sixgun when her head struck the ground. Now, she struggled to her feet and staggered toward her horse, knowing she could not possibly grab her Winchester and bring the bull down before she was impaled on the deadly horns.

Jessie turned to face her death, but then Ki leaped out of the brush, and his *surushin* was spinning across the clearing. The six foot length of rope with its two leather-covered steel balls made a whirring sound as they drove to the forelegs of the bull and wrapped themselves around the animal's hocks. The bull's legs seemed to bend like broken sticks as its foamy muzzle struck the earth. Its momentum sent the huge animal into a somersault and Jessie had but an instant to see the sun blot out before the bull's body crashed down. She tried to leap out of the way but one of her legs did not seem to respond. Jessie felt blinding pain, and then something like a ball of light burst behind her eyes and she fell spinning into a well of darkness.

Chapter 2

The samurai went straight to Jessica and knelt beside her. He quickly took her pulse, and though his face did not reveal the full measure of his relief, he looked up at the Circle Star foreman and nodded.

"Thank God!" Ed Wright whispered. "If you didn't always wrap those two damned balls on the ends of a rope around your waist, nothing short of a Sharps buffalo rifle would have brought that bull down before it ripped out her belly."

"She'll be all right. Probably wake up in a few minutes, mad as anything but ready to get back in the saddle and go after another one."

"But Sun won't be." The foreman walked over to inspect the stallion's wounds. "Another couple of inches lower and deeper and this horse of hers would be a goner. Jess?"

A lean cowboy rode up. "Yeah?"

"Ride back to the ranch and doctor this horse. On your way back, bring a buckboard for Miss Starbuck in case she's a little more banged up than Ki thinks she is."

"Yes sir, Mr. Wright," Jess said.

8

Ki shrugged. "We won't need the buckboard. Miss Starbuck would rather be tied across her saddle than carried away from her roundup in a wagon."

"I know that," Ed grumped. "You and her are both about as stubborn as a pair of mules. But try to talk some sense into her when she wakes up. I'm just glad her pa ain't alive to see how we fell down on our job here today. I sure wish that girl would quit cowboyin' and stick to doin' whatever it is you and her do on all those business trips."

"Cowboying relaxes her," Ki said, walking to his horse and getting his canteen. He wetted a cloth, and when he returned, he gently dabbed at his employer's face. "She would much rather be in the saddle than in a boardroom."

"Well," Ed muttered grudgingly. "I know that, but she makes it a little hard for the men to concentrate on what they're supposed to do. You remember last week how Billy Edgar was watching her instead of which direction his horse was a-gallopin'?"

"I remember," Ki said, suppressing a grin. Billy had almost beheaded himself on a low-hanging tree branch. The doctor had said it was a miracle that he hadn't broken his fool neck.

"And how last month, in Austin, Miss Starbuck rode down the street and created a stampede on the barber shops and bath houses?"

"She can't help the way she looks," Ki said.

"Yeah, I know that," Ed said. "But she's so pretty even an ugly old fella like me gets rattled when she smiles. Foolishness, I know. But Lord, she sure is a beauty."

It was true, Ki thought. Even with dirt smeared across her cheeks and in her hair, Jessie was a strikingly beautiful woman. She had green eyes that reminded him of the rarest Oriental jade. Her hair was copper-blond, and it shone in

9

the Texas sun when she rode horseback. Her cheekbones were unusually high for a Caucasian woman, and she was long-limbed and full-breasted. Ki, being half Caucasian and half Japanese, had thought that a woman as lovely and delicate-appearing as this could not possibly also be gifted with character, humility, and strength. But he had quickly discovered that he was wrong. Jessica Starbuck was one of those rare beauties who paid no attention at all to her physical attractiveness. She ran an empire, and she did it with the same intelligence, drive, and dedication that her father had exhibited throughout his lifetime.

"Damn that bull!" Ed grated, twisting around to look at the thrashing animal. He stomped over to his horse and yanked his .30-.30 rifle from his boot and levered a shell into the chamber. "I ought to kill this big bastard slow with bullets to the belly, but I can't rightly do that, so I'll finish him off quick."

The samurai shook his head emphatically. "No. She wanted that bull alive. If you kill it, she will have risked her life for nothing. She would want the animal branded and castrated like all the others."

Ed pulled off his soiled and shapeless Stetson as several more Circle Star cowboys rode in fast only to discover that the action was all finished. The ranch foreman frowned as he studied the bull. "You sure, Ki?"

"Yes."

"Well then, I'll take your word for it. You know how she thinks better than I do. But if it's all the same to you, I want to do the castrating myself. I haven't sharpened my knife for a couple of days, but the dull sonofabitch oughta be worthy of sawin' off this big fella's balls."

Ki nodded. He understood the ranch foreman and knew that it might be necessary, in Ed Wright's mind, to extract some kind of retribution for what the longhorn had done to Jessica Starbuck.

Ed turned to the cowboys. "Some of you go scrounge up some kindling wood and get me a branding iron. This is one case of surgery that I am surely going to enjoy botching up a little. Boys, throw a couple more loops around his front and hind legs and stretch him out real good for me."

The cowboys were already shaking out their loops. In moments, they had the bull hung out like a wash-line. Ed knelt between the animal's legs and hefted the monstrous scrotum. He grinned and pulled out his pocket knife. With more satisfaction than the job deserved, he slashed into the scrotum and the longhorn bellowed. He sliced a four-inch incision and reached inside the sack and pulled out the testicles. Then, he placed the bloodied blade of his knife to the white cords that fed them and cut them off cleanly. It was done quickly and without malice. Despite his personal feelings, Ed Wright was one of the finest cattlemen in Texas, and all business when it came to such things. The job was done so efficiently that the animal hardly bled.

Ten minutes later, Ed took the cherry-red branding iron and slapped it against the steer's brindle coat. The animal shuddered, bawled weakly, and slapped its horns up and down on the grass.

"You cut off their balls," one cowboy said, "they're suddenly all a bunch of pussycats."

"You'd be wearin' a damned petticoat if we took off yours, Ernie," another cowboy said with a slow grin.

Ed pulled the branding iron back from the steer's hide as smoke lifted over the sage. He set the iron down and unwrapped Ki's *surushin*. "I'll never kid you about carrying this damned thing around your waist again," he said. "I

11

never thought I'd see the day when a rope and two leather-covered steel balls could do what a rifle could not."

Ki took the *surushin* and went back to attend to Jessie. He poured more water from his canteen and patted her face until her eyes fluttered open. She looked at the samurai and shook her head. "I guess I probably caused you and Ed a scare, huh?"

She tried to sit up but he gently held her down for a moment longer. "Your horse will be all right. Just a few gouges and scratches. But we had one of the boys take him back to the ranch house for doctoring. Ed also thought it would be best if you rode back to headquarters in a buck-board."

Jessie's green eyes flashed. "Oh you did, did you?" she exclaimed, pushing Ki's restraining hand away and sitting up. "Well, in that case, Mr. Wright, I think I'll use one of the cowboy's horses and let them go back early. Let's get to moving! We've still got a roundup to finish!"

Ki stepped back and winked at the Circle Star ranch foreman. Ed grinned. "I reckon you really are feeling all right again, Miss Starbuck."

"Of course I am." She walked over to the longhorn steer and shook her head a little sadly.

And though Jessie did not say a word, she wanted the animal to understand that she did not bear it any ill will. It had been fighting to hold what it had fought other bulls to claim—more cows, more range. And when tracked into the chaparral, it had retreated to finally stand its ground—the way a person should when outnumbered and hunted by his enemies.

"Let him up and drive him in with the herd," Jessie said, brushing the dirt from her hair and clothes. She glanced up at the sun. "Let's ride. We still have six hours of daylight and a bunch more almost as big as this one to shag out of the brush."

Ed Wright gave the signal and all the cowboys but the most recently hired swung into their saddles.

As they started off into the brush, Jessie held her new horse in for a moment and looked at the man whose mount she had claimed. "I'm sorry to leave you stranded like this, Jim. But I need to be out there with my men."

Jim Sanders yanked his hat off. He was tall, in his twenties, and already nearly bald, a fact that the cowboys never let him forget. Bashful and unused to any boss apologizing for anything, he stammered, "It's your range, your beef and your horse, ma'am."

"I know that," Jessie said. "But it's your saddle. And I'll take care of it."

"I know that, ma'am."

Jessie started to rein away, then hesitated. "Jim?"

"Yes, ma'am!"

"Even if that brindle is castrated, I'd still keep those last two ropes around his fore and hind legs until you have a buckboard to get up into. No sense in taking unnecessary risks."

"Yes ma'am." He summoned up his courage. "I would respectfully offer the same advice to you, Miss Starbuck."

Jessie nodded and then said, "Yes. Sometimes I'm afraid I'm better at giving advice than taking it. Thanks for reminding me, Jim."

The cowboy's face flushed red with embarrassment and his adam's apple bobbed up and down. Seeing how much her compliment had flustered the shy cowboy, Jessie smiled and rode away.

* * *

Four days later, Jessie and Ki returned to Circle Star headquarters. Jessie had been reluctant to leave the roundup, but common sense told her that the operation was in very capable hands under her experienced ranch foreman.

"He'll probably get along better and get more work accomplished than with me there breathing over his shoulder," Jessie said as they rode into the ranch yard. "But I sure do enjoy the roundup more than sitting at a desk and handling paperwork. Still, I have to see how Sun is doing."

Ki nodded and stepped down from his pinto. Seeing him dismount and head into the barn, Jessie was once again impressed by what a fine physical specimen of manhood he was. Ki was of a little above average in height but appeared deceptively small because of his slender build. He probably did not weigh over 160 pounds, but every ounce of it was hard muscle and bone. His hair was black, slightly longer than that of a regular cowboy, and he wore a headband. His eyes were dark brown, large, and almond-shaped. Ki looked and moved like nothing more or less than a mountain lion. He was fluid in motion, graceful beyond anything Jessie had ever seen in a man. And, she suspected, he treasured her in a way that transcended lust or the simple loyalty one might expect from a devoted employee. Ki was her protector, her best friend; for those reasons and many more, Jessie knew he could never be her lover. A samurai never confused loyalty with passion. To do so would be to lose honor.

She found Sun in a stall, and the stallion greeted her with a soft nicker. Jessie moved in and inspected the beautiful animal. "I'm sorry I got you into a tight fix," she told the palomino, stroking its muscular neck. "I know that you didn't have any chance in the middle of that damned chaparral. I'll be more careful next time."

The stallion bobbed its head as if in understanding. Jessie's hand smoothed over each place where the bull's wicked horns had cut and torn hide. "The scars will probably fill in with white hair," she said. "But I don't give a darn about that."

"You were both very lucky," Ki said.

Jessie shook her head. "Luck had a lot less to do with it than you did."

She scratched the horse behind the ear for a few minutes before leaving. "Let's have an early dinner," she told Ki as she started toward the elegant house her father had built many years ago.

Circle Star headquarters was shaded by massive cottonwood and oak trees planted by her father long ago. There were barns, corrals, a cookshack, a bunkhouse big enough for forty with its own covered porch for the boys to sit on in the evenings and yarn to each other, and a well-equipped blacksmith's shop, where a blacksmith and a wheelwright worked full time just to keep the horses shod and the wagons in good repair.

Men waved and smiled in greeting as she marched toward the house. Some of them were old and bent, unable to do any more hard riding, but Jessie would keep them on her payroll until they died. She valued loyalty above everything else, and no cowboy or vaquero who risked his life and limb on the Circle Star ranch for years would ever starve or have to go to some festering city's poorhouse.

The moment Jessie walked inside, the coolness and beauty of the huge adobe and rock home enveloped her with memories. The walls seemed soaked with her father's

15

laughter, which had carried through the great hallways and permeated every room. The house itself was of gigantic proportions because Alex Starbuck had been a builder and had loved to add new rooms. Downstairs was the great marble and Spanish-tiled living room with its slate fireplace that reached from floor to ceiling. It was big enough to devour entire tree stumps. How many wonderful nights had they spent discussing the world and its intricate politics and rich cultures? A hundred, or a thousand? Ki had always been a part of those discussions; he was as much a brother to her as a friend.

Jessie greeted one of the maids and then passed through the spacious dining room with its glistening wood floor and mahogany table with a dozen carved wooden chairs imported from France. The ceilings were supported by exposed roof-timbers of massive proportions.

Several of her employees offered greetings and she answered each one with a smile.

"Are you all right?" a pretty Mexican girl asked, studying her dirty clothes and a faint dark bruise on one cheek earned from her recent spill off Sun.

"I'm just fine, Carmelita. What is for dinner?"

"Roast beef, potatoes, and peaches. For dessert, your favorite apple cobbler."

"Mmmm. Sounds wonderful. Chuckwagon cooking can get old in a hurry. And I'm afraid I do get weary of the sand and dirt that always seem to get into the food. Please ask the kitchen to make up enough cobbler to take back to the roundup crew in the morning."

Carmelita nodded. "That will make the cowboy and vaqueros very happy, Miss Starbuck."

"But not the kitchen, eh?" Jessie said with a wink that make the Mexican maid giggle and nod her head.

16

Jessie went to her study with its great library shelves, which contained books that ranged from Shakespeare to *The Physics of Building Modern Paddlewheel Steam Vessels*. At the huge old oak desk her father had used for more than twenty years to juggle his fortunes in all parts of the world, Jessie found a disappointingly tall stack of letters and reports that required her immediate attention. All were opened but unread.

Gauging the stack and thumbing through it hurriedly before she went up and had a bath in preparation for dinner, Jessie frowned. She glanced at the grandfather clock nearby and knew that she would have to work far into the night. There were at least thirty business letters to answer, including financial reports from Asia and South Africa that would require some very careful analysis. Equally important were pages and price quotations from a German steel-rail maker and a Philadelphia railroad engine builder, giving her costs of rolling stock she was considering buying for one of her biggest rubber plantations in Malaysia.

Each decision would be weighed carefully, and only after she had read all the reports from her field managers with their supporting facts would she answer. Jessie noticed that a speculative silver mine in Bolivia seemed to be on the verge of paying off handsomely but would require about fifty thousand more dollars in developmental costs.

She might give her manager thirty and a warning to cut all overhead expenses until the operation began to make a profit. As rich as he had eventually become, Alex Starbuck had taught his daughter never to take wealth for granted. Money was like water in that it could easily drown you, or drain away through the fingers of your hand.

But tomorrow, she intended to be back on Sun and headed for the roundup.

* * *

The grandfather clock was chiming three o'clock in the morning when she finished all her business correspondence. Jessie rubbed her tired eyes and neatly stacked all her reply letters for her secretary to post. Finally, she allowed herself the reward of glancing at the waiting stack of personal letters. She knew she should wait to read them later in the morning, but they were a reward for going through her business mail. Alex had taught her to always save good things until last.

The first letters she glanced at were from old friends scattered throughout the world. A senator from Kentucky, a Belgian prince, the owner of a small shop in Vienna who made exquisite jewelry. But there was one letter posted from a Michael D. Bodie, in Skull Creek, Wyoming, that she simply could not place.

Her first thought before opening it was that her secretary had probably misfiled the letter as personal when in fact it should have been forwarded to one of her business managers, because it was sure to be a request for employment. But when Jessica opened the letter and began to read, she realized she could not have been more mistaken. The letter read:

Dear Miss Starbuck, I am sure you do not remember me, and there is no reason that you should. But I am the son of your late father's friend, Pete Bodie. My father, as you might recall, once saved your father's life in the China Sea during a typhoon, the year, I think, being around 1840. I write to ask your help on behalf of my father who is in jail and will surely be hanged though he is an innocent man —as I also am innocent. What then, you might ask,

18

are we being persecuted so wrongly for? For being sheepmen, Miss Starbuck, in a cattle kingdom. My father and I are accused of murder. The evidence is pure fabrication but it will hang us nevertheless. I ask your help, not for myself, but for the decent man who once saved your father's life thus enabling him to build the vast empire and wealth you now command. We have no other possibility or hope. Come quickly, the trial begins very soon and I cannot allow my father to die without some immediate retribution. Sincerely, Michael D. Bodie, a sheepman on the run.

Jessie found herself instantly wide awake. She reread the letter over and over. Then she replaced it in its envelope and went up to bed. But sleep eluded her despite her weariness. And as soon as dawn tinged the eastern horizon with salmon-and-gold-colored fingers, she arose and headed for the small guest house where the samurai lived alone and according to his own Oriental customs and beliefs.

She found Ki sitting crosslegged on a mat made of rice stems. He was meditating, eyes closed, head thrown back, his bare torso and strong face illuminated with the colors of sunrise. Jessie hesitated a moment and almost turned away, for she did not want to disturb him at such a time.

But he was aware of her presence and said, "You bless me so early this morning for something very important. Is this wrong?"

Jessie shook her head and went around to face him. "I have received a letter that I want you to read."

She gave him the letter and watched him read it slowly. "Well?"

19

"What do you want me to say?" he asked. "You have already decided that we should go and I fully agree."

"How do you know I haven't decided to send our best lawyer and several investigators?"

"Because," Ki said, "this is a personal matter that involves a friend of your father's. You would never allow such a matter to rest in the hands of anyone but yourself."

"I'll need you."

"Of course. It is my karma to go where you go—always."

Jessie saw the samurai close his eyes again, fold his strong arms across his chest, and turn his face to the rising sun.

She did not even have to tell this man when he needed to be ready to leave. He would know that too.

They were leaving for Wyoming within the hour.

Chapter 3

Because of the absence of a train heading north out of Texas, it took them a week to reach Pueblo, Colorado, by stagecoach. Jessie and Ki then boarded the Denver and Rio Grande Western Railroad north for Denver. In that city, they would connect with the Union Pacific, which would carry them all the way to Rock Springs, Wyoming. From Rock Springs, they would have less than a hundred miles left to reach Skull Creek.

Now, as they pulled into Denver and prepared to disembark and await their connection, Jessie felt unusually tired and filled with worry. "They might even have hung the man by now," she said.

"Then you should not be concerned, for we can do nothing. But even if the father is dead, perhaps we can still save the son."

"What if they've already hunted him down and he's buried too?"

Ki shrugged philosophically. It was not in the samurai tradition to fret about something that he could not change. Ki considered such things as a man's karma. His life force, his past, and his present, were all intertwined in the totality

21

of his existence. To a samurai's way of reasoning, you could not change karma, only accept it with tranquility. Jessie had heard this explanation several times, but she did not buy the logic. Dozens of times, men had tried to kill her or her samurai, and Ki always fought with deadly intensity.

Maybe, she thought, Ki believed his karma was to defeat all of their enemies.

"I telegraphed Joe Beals and he is supposed to be packed and ready to leave at once. He's one of the finest lawyers that Starbuck Enterprises has ever hired. I used him in a sticky bit of litigation up at Leadville."

"I remember that," Ki said. "He won our case with a brilliant and very novel approach to mining law."

"Yes. But I'm a little worried. He's in his sixties now, and his health isn't all that good. I'd feel terrible if this additional strain of helping the Bodies should further endanger his condition."

"Maybe he has a younger man he can recommend."

But Jessie shook her head. "I want the very best that money can buy. Besides, Mr. Beals has connections up in Wyoming that I might not have. If it's true that old Pete Bodie is being stampeded simply because he's a sheepman, then it's possible even the judge up there is unethical."

Ki agreed. "It'll be a small town—a cattle town. And you know how they feel about sheep."

"I know." Jessie shook her head. "It's ironic, isn't it? Me, Jessica Starbuck, one of the biggest cattle ranchers in Southwest Texas, coming to defend a sheepman. I detest sheep!"

"Do you know much about them?" Ki asked with a half-smile.

"No," she admitted. "Well, I know as much as I ever

22

want to. Sheep yank the grass out by the roots and leave their wool's grease on it so that cattle can't hardly tolerate the taste of it. Sheep bleat and stink. They're stupid and noisy and—"

"Whoa!" Ki said, leaning out of his seat in the first-class coach that they occupied. "I know you don't like them, but in Japan, mutton and lamb are considered to be superior to beef or veal."

Jessie's face reflected her shock and disbelief.

"That's right," the samurai said. "And wool is prized for its warmth and durability. You can't weave with the hair off a cow."

"That's ridiculous!"

"Maybe. I'm only pointing out to you that there are two points of view."

"You sound as if you're already turning sheepman."

Ki grinned. "I'm always for the underdog, just as you are, Jessie. If the Bodies are innocent, we'll want to stop an injustice."

"We may be walking right into the middle of a range war," Jessie said as she felt the train slow and pull up to the train station in Denver.

Denver had grown, even in the year since she had last visited it. Without question, Denver was now the largest city between St. Louis and the Pacific coast. It was ideally situated right at the junction of the Great Plains and the Rocky Mountains. As such, it enjoyed a huge amount of freighting, farming, and ranching commerce. And when cattle or wheat prices fell, it seemed as if the nearby lumber and mining payrolls were always ready to fill in and support the city's businesses.

"Do you see Mr. Beals?" Jessie asked anxiously.

Ki shook his head as a large crowd pressed forward on the platform to greet arriving passengers. "Not yet."

"I'll bet anything he is sick."

"Don't be so pessimistic."

"I'm not pessimistic. Realistic is closer to the mark," Jessie said. "I should have summoned Mark Pettit from San Francisco. He's good. Not brilliant, and he doesn't know a soul in Wyoming, but he's one of the best courtroom lawyers I have ever seen. Mark can bring a jury to tears, or whip them up to a hanging fury. He plays a jury like a musical instrument."

"I like Mr. Beals better for this job," Ki said. "Having contacts in Wyoming could well prove to be the deciding factor."

"Yes." Jessie scowled as she prepared to disembark from the train. "But the fact that he is not out there to greet us right now does not bode well."

When they stepped down onto the train platform, they were suddenly confronted by a young man who was badly winded from an obviously long run. He looked to be in his mid-twenties, and his hair was sandy-colored, rather longish, and parted down the middle. His spectacles were so thick that they made his eyes seem enormous. His best feature was his strong jaw and a luxurious handlebar mustache, but even that was knocked out of kilter. He was tall and angular, and when he spoke, he was so badly out of breath that his voice came out in short gasps.

"Miss . . . Starbuck!"

"Yes. Who are you?"

"William Lamar," he wheezed, "at your service!"

He bowed so suddenly that he might have cracked his forehead against Jessie's had she not jumped back in time. "Who are you?" Jessie repeated.

"William Lamar at your service!" he repeated in that same wheezing gasp. "If you allow me to catch my breath, I'll explain everything to your satisfaction."

"That," Ki said skeptically, "I doubt."

They gave the young man several minutes to gather his composure. Young Lamar ran his fingers nervously through his tousled blond hair and removed his glasses which had become badly foggged due to his exertions.

"All right, Mr. Lamar," Jessie said impatiently. "I think Ki and I can assume you were sent by Mr. Beals to meet us. Is he ill?"

"Worse," Lamar said solemnly.

"How much worse?"

"He's dead."

Jessie groaned. "I'm sorry to hear that. When did he pass away?"

"This morning, on the way to your train."

"My God!" Jessie cried. "I hope I had nothing to do with it."

Lamar shrugged his wide but bony shoulders. "I should think not," he said. "Mr. Beals was a dying man. Heart condition. But I guess maybe that running for this train— we were late—well, that might have caused his heart to burst."

Jessie stared bleakly at the crowd. "We can't even wait for the funeral," she lamented. "We have an emergency in Skull Creek, Wyoming."

"I know that," William said. "That's why I'm here. You see, Mr. Beals knew that he wasn't fit to travel so he asked me to take his place."

"You?" Even Ki could not hide his disbelief.

"That's right." Larmar had enough spirit to show that he

25

was offended. "I'm his nephew and a very fine attorney, sir!"

"How long have you practiced?"

Lamar deflated like a punctured balloon. "Not terribly long, but . . . but I've admired my uncle all my life. I spent years as a child watching him destroy his opponents in the courtroom. He tutored me. Taught me the law according to the statutes of Colorado Territory, and I know it backwards and forwards. I can actually quote chapters and—"

Jessie gripped the young man's skinny arm. "Mr. Lamar, we don't mean any disrespect. But what we are facing in Wyoming is a *murder* trial. The lives of two innocent men are at stake. This is not a case for a neophyte, a young man who seeks to test his newfound knowledge in the courtroom."

"But . . . but I have a letter from my uncle. He knew that I could do the job. I've been studying range law and homicide cases every hour since your telegram arrived. We even pretended to be a judge, accused, and jury, and prepared for every possible argument."

"Why don't you show Miss Starbuck the letter?"

"The what?"

"The letter!" Jessie said with growing impatience.

"Oh, yes." Lamar shoved a big hand inside his coat and then his face paled. "It's gone!" He began to slap his coat and search madly through his pockets. "My uncle's letter of introduction is gone! I must have lost it on the run over here, or at the funeral parlor!"

Jessie shook her head. "Mr. Lamar," she said, "I know you're well-intentioned, and I'm sure that you would do your very best, but—"

"Please!" he begged. "You don't understand that this is the opportunity of a lifetime for me! My uncle understood

26

what it would mean for my career if only you would let me represent your friends."

"Don't you understand?" Jessie asked with growing exasperation. "This is a life and death situation."

"For me as well as the Bodies!" Lamar cried. "Miss Starbuck. Mr. Ki. If you'll only give me the chance, I swear I'll save those sheepmen if they are innocent. I even like mutton!"

If the situation had not been so pathetic and desperate, Jessie would have smiled, relented, and taken the young man along. But she could not afford to allow her sympathy for William Lamar to color her judgment.

"I'm sorry. I'm sure you mean well, but we must have someone with experience. Please, can you be so kind as to recommend another Denver attorney that might take this case on a moment's notice? Our train leaves in one hour."

"There's no one else," Lamar said triumphantly. "No one at all."

"There is always someone if the price is right," Jessie said. "I'll pay very well."

"I'll do it for free!"

"No!"

Lamar sagged with defeat. "My life is in ashes at your feet, Miss Starbuck. I am ruined."

"Nonsense," she told him sharply. "You're being overly dramatic."

"I'll come whether you hire me or not," he said in a voice that shook with fervor. "You cannot stop me from coming to Skull Creek and trying to help!"

Jessie sighed. "I don't have time to argue with you. And it's true that I can't stop you from boarding this train and coming to Skull Creek. But I wish you'd reconsider. I'm sure that your late uncle has clients who will need your immediate services. There must be matters to which you can address your legal training and be of great benefit here in Denver."

"I'm coming," he said, ignoring her words, "because ... because I want to work for Starbuck Enterprises and become the best lawyer you have ever hired."

Jessie was touched and impressed. She glanced at Ki and saw that he was similarly impressed. "Listen," she said. "On our return trip, I promise I will stop by to pay my respects to your dear aunt and to talk to you about future employment with Starbuck. I'm always looking for dedicated lawyers who are unafraid of new challenges that I might send them to face in any part of the world."

"I'm not afraid of anything in a courtroom," he blurted with pride.

"I know that. Now please give me the names of Denver's two best attorneys and show me to their offices at once."

Lamar nodded his head. "All right," he sighed. "Follow me."

"I'll make sure our luggage and things are taken care of," Ki said. "And that they get on the train to Cheyenne."

Jessie nodded. She had a suitcase full of important papers to go over, and another that contained five thousand dollars in cash. She was not taking a chance that there would be no bank in Skull Creek. And though she would never attempt to buy or bribe a jury, Jessie knew that money could go a long way toward turning up beneficial evidence on behalf of her client.

As they left the train station it occurred to Jessie that young William Lamar was sort of dragging his heels. He talked about the weather and a number of inconsequential things until Jessie said with exasperation, "Can't we hurry? I have less than forty-five minutes!"

Lamar apologized and stretched his long legs out enough to make Jessie hurry. They walked clear into the center of town, and the attorney took them to the office of L. L. Dewey, Attorney at Law.

"Are you sure he's good?"

"Yes."

"Well, thank you."

"I'll wait right here outside his door in case he doesn't want to go to Wyoming in forty minutes," Lamar said with a sly grin.

"Do that," Jessie snapped as she walked into the office. One foot inside, she was immediately engulfed with the vilest cigar smoke she had ever had the misfortune to inhale. The stuff was blue and noxious, and it filled the room from the ceiling down to the desktops.

Jessie bent down and saw a seedy looking man sitting at a desk that had a plaque with the nameplate L. L. DEWEY.

When he saw Jessie, he immediately came to his feet and his face was obscured in the hateful cloud of smoke. "Can I help you, miss?" he asked, cigar clenched between his tobacco-stained teeth.

"No," Jessie said, reaching a quick but easy decision and heading for the door. "A mistake has been made."

The man's face reflected disappointment. He started forward, but Jessie was out the door and into the hallway, moving fast, before he could cross the room.

"What happened?" Lamar asked.

"You didn't warn me about his cigar smoke! My father smoked cigars, but not the kind of weeds he smokes. I almost got sick in there!"

"I'm sorry."

"Don't apologize," Jessie said. "Just find me a good lawyer! One who has a nice office that reflects some level of professional success!"

"Yes, Miss Starbuck," Lamar said obediently.

The office of Daniel Stout was opulent. The floors were covered with expensive rugs and the walls were of polished walnut with expensive oil paintings of cowboys, cattle, and horses. Mr. Stout had a spacious room in the best part of town, and the moment that Jessie met him, she had the feeling of hope. He was warm, handsome, confident looking.

"Mr. Stout," she began, "I have an emergency in Skull Creek, Wyoming. I need you to come with me on today's train."

His jaw actually dropped, but before he could say anything, Jessie said, "I am prepared to pay you twice your normal fee."

The jaw clamped shut. "When does the train leave?"

She consulted her watch. "In a little less than thirty minutes."

"Impossible! But perhaps I could catch the next train."

"No," she said firmly. "You must come now. The trial may have already begun. I'll pay you *triple* your normal fee."

"I suppose I could grab a bag and leave a note for my wife. In a sentence or two, what is this case about?"

"You will represent two sheepherders against a valley full of Wyoming cattlemen. It sounds like a range war. Some of the cattlemen have apparently framed two innocent sheepmen for murder."

Stout rose to his feet and said stiffly, "I'm afraid I am not your man, miss. . . ."

"Why not!" she cried with exasperation.

"Because," he said through clenched teeth, "I just happen to be the president of the Colorado Cattlemen's Association. And I hate sheepmen! Good day, miss."

Now Jessie's jaw dropped, then clamped shut. "Damn that William!" she swore in a fury. "I'm out of time and I'll kill him!"

Stout turned his back on her, and on her way out Jessie slammed his office door so hard it sounded like a rifle shot. When she saw William Lamar standing in the hallway with a weak grin on his face, she almost attacked him.

"All right!" she said tightly. "Now I've run out of time and patience and have no choice but to take you. But you had better be good!"

He beamed—did everything but dance a jig. Then, offering Jessie his arm (which she ignored), they headed for the train on the run.

They barely made it. When they swung up onto the train, it was starting to move. Ki was standing at the foot of the platform, and he helped the out-of-breath Jessie to her seat.

"Cutting it mighty fine, aren't you?" he asked with a smile.

"A little. Ki, I want you to meet Starbuck's newest attorney. The man that is going to present a brilliant defense for the Bodies."

Ki looked at William Lamar and shook his head. Even though he was not more than five or six years older than the attorney, there was something about Ki that gave the bearing of maturity beyond his years. But now, as he viewed William Lamar, he was obviously hard pressed to find anything encouraging to say except "Welcome aboard. It ought to be interesting."

Lamar removed his fogged spectacles and cleaned them

with his handkerchief. He looked as flushed and excited as a schoolboy on his first hayride.

"You won't be sorry," he pledged.

"Of course not," Ki said. "But then *we* aren't the ones that are being accused of murder."

Lamar nodded, conceding the point. "I sure wish I'd had the time to bring along my law books," he fretted. "I had all kinds of legal cases underlined that might be relevant."

Jessie looked sharply at the lawyer. "What about all those legal cases you swore you could recite from memory?"

Lamar bit his fingernails. "I sort of . . . well, I just might have exaggerated," he admitted.

"Did you also exaggerate when you said that you were qualified to practice law?"

"Oh no, ma'am! My uncle said I had one of the finest legal minds he had ever seen at my stage of development." Lamar sat up straight in his seat and straightened his tie. He gazed around the train coach. It was clear he had never even traveled by rail before. Jessie shook her head. Young Lamar was really going to be a nice looking man when he matured and filled out a little. Trouble was, his "stage of development" might not be equal to what awaited them in Wyoming.

Chapter 4

As the train steamed out of Denver, a sheriff and three deputies came tromping through their first-class coach on their way toward the rear of the train. They gave Jessie, Ki, and Lamar a quick once-over glance and then passed on without a word.

"What do you suppose that was about?" Jessie asked.

"No one has said anything, but I have the feeling," Ki mused aloud, "that there is a lot of money being carried aboard this train."

"To where?"

Ki shrugged. "I heard some talk that there was a big land and cattle sale up in Cheyenne. The two might be connected."

Lamar nodded thoughtfully. "There was a big writeup in the Denver papers about a ranch sale. I'll bet you have it right, Ki."

Jessie turned back to study the country. The grass waved in the afternoon sun and the land was rolling to the east, but, to the west, the mighty Rocky Mountains humped boldly toward a forever sky. This was pretty fair cattle country, but also surprisingly rich under the plow. Winter wheat, oats, and barley did well here, and so did corn. Everything depended on the amount of rainfall and the length of the summer. Denver could have snow on the ground as early as October.

The samurai stood up in his seat. "I think I'll go back and just find out what is going on."

"We haven't had a train robbery on this line in two years," Lamar said.

Ki was not impressed. "Do you happen to remember the amount of the Cheyenne sale?"

"Sure. Eighty thousand dollars. It was the biggest land sale in Wyoming's history. The buyer lives right here in Denver."

Ki's eyes met Jessie's. "Eighty thousand dollars is enough temptation for every outlaw within a thousand miles. The trip to Cheyenne is only a hundred miles. I think I'll find a place where I could be of more help."

"Good idea," Jessie said.

They watched the samurai head down the aisle. When he was gone, Lamar said, "He never relaxes for a minute, does he?"

"No. He's the most vigilant man I've ever known."

"Where does he come from?"

"Japan. His father was an American seaman. His mother was Japanese, of royal blood. Because she dared to marry out of her race and culture, she was shamed and cast out of her society. Ki's father intended to bring his infant son and his bride to America. Unfortunately, he died of illness, and the mother soon followed. Ki was left alone to fend for himself. He was an outcast. Half white, half Japanese, he became a starving beggar—an object of ridicule."

"My God!" Lamar said, glancing back toward the door

through which the samurai had vanished. "Then how did he ever get out of such a miserable condition?"

Jessie loved the story, and she knew that Ki would not mind her relating it now. "Ki was very young, perhaps eight or nine years old when he met an old *ronin*—"

"A what?"

"*Ronin*. It is Japanese, and means a samurai whose master has died. Without a master to serve, a samurai's entire purpose, his very reason for existence, is over."

"Is that how he thinks of you? As his master?"

Jessie shook her head. "Ki is free to come or go. He chooses to help me, as he chose to help my father. But that is getting ahead of the story."

"Yes," Lamar said, "but before we change the subject, I sense that Ki is more to you than just an employee."

"He is my best and truest friend."

"I sense he is even more than that."

Jessie's green eyes hardened. "He is not my lover, if that is what—"

"Oh no!" Lamar cried with consternation. "Forgive me, Miss Starbuck. That was not what I was thinking. I . . . what a fool I am making of myself! I just thought that he seemed so . . ."

Jessie's anger vanished as fast as it had risen in her. "So what?"

"So . . . dedicated. Yes," Lamar said enthusiastically, "he seems totally dedicated to you and your welfare."

Jessie looked right at the young attorney. "Total commitment—without being asked—will bring you success beyond your greatest dreams in the Starbuck empire. I never demand obedience from my top people. But I do expect them to represent me and my companies as

35

members of an elite and totally professional team. And always with honor."

"Yes, ma'am." Lamar took a deep breath, and his face reflected unhappiness. "You should know that since your telegram came to my uncle and he showed it to me, I have read everything I could find about you, Ki, and the Starbuck empire. You're both legendary. I feel—"

"Please," Jessie said quietly.

"Okay, but I want you to know how much I admire you and the samurai. I just wish that he did not regard me with such total contempt."

Jessie's voice softened. "You are wrong. Ki measures everyone by a simple standard. Words mean little to him, only deeds. He will judge you as he judges all people—by your actions."

"Is that how the *ronin* taught him?"

"Yes," Jessie said. "The man's name was Hirata. I have never heard Ki speak of him except with the greatest respect. He was a mountain of dignity and strength. He tested Ki's bravery and found it equal to the lessons he had to teach. And, over many years, he taught Ki everything. They called it *kakuto bugei,* 'the true samurai's way.' He can kill a man easier and faster with his hands and feet than most lawmen can with a Colt .45. And he saved my life dozens of times."

"What happened to the old *ronin?*"

"He committed *seppuku,* which means suicide by ritual disembowelment."

Lamar's eyes grew round and even larger as the realization of what she was saying sank home. "You mean he used a knife or something and opened himself up?"

"Yes," Jessie said quietly. "That too is the true samurai way."

36

"Jesus," Lamar whispered. "Would Ki really do something like that?"

Jessie chose not to answer. If she were ever slain by an enemy, she was very certain that Ki *would* commit seppuku.

"Why don't we talk about you and the troubles that await us in Skull Creek?" she said, changing the subject.

Lamar seemed to understand that he had touched on something very deep and sacred between Jessica Starbuck and her samurai. "Of course," he said quietly. "And if I have pried, I'm—"

"If you had pried I would have told you so. Now," Jessie added, "let's talk law and range wars."

"Okay," he said. "To begin with, all of that part of Wyoming is either federal land or homesteaded. Now, the statutes on homestead law in the Wyoming Territory read: 'Whosoever shall put upon the land, in such as to leave clear definition of title, and whosoever shall have that land surveyed and recorded with . . .'"

Jessie smiled inwardly to herself. At least, she thought, as the young attorney droned on, he really does have quite a memory for legal documents. Now if only he can present the law persuasively in a courtroom, perhaps we will have a fighting chance.

Ki sat in the last coach before the baggage compartment and pretended to scan an old Denver newspaper that someone had left lying on one of the worn wooden seats.

This was the third-class coach, and the differences between it and Jessie's first-class accomodations could not have been more striking. In this coach, the passengers rode on rough wooden benches. Some were splintered, most

37

had names and initials carved in them, and all were extremely uncomfortable.

The coach itself was dirty, the floors littered, and the windows cracked or broken. Men spat tobacco on the walls and floors for lack of cuspidors or good manners. Women, dressed in shapeless calico dresses, hugged squawling babies, and the smell of cigar smoke and liquor was heavy. Drunks snored under the benches and an old Indian woman hugged her knees and rocked back and forth on the floor.

The coach was packed with a motley collection that included miners, sod-busters, down-and-out gamblers and a few hung-over or busted up cowboys, who played poker for matchsticks and beans. Designed to hold about fifty passengers, the coach was jammed with at least seventy. Some men slept while others stood and stared out the dirty, smoke-smeared windows. There were pot-bellied stoves at each end and a small outhouse with nothing but a hole in the seat where excrement dropped on the blurring rails as the train sped north.

It was grim, but very cheap. For a little more than two dollars, a man could ride from Denver to Cheyenne in about three hours. By horse or coach, it took a full day of hard traveling.

"Hey, Chinaman! Get the hell on the floor where you belong. The seats are for white men, not celestials and niggers!"

Ki stiffened. On the frontier, where men were supposed to be manly only if they wore beards, smoked cigars, and wore guns on their hips, he was constantly being challenged by bigoted idiots like the barrel-chested man who stood before him.

"Hey!" the man growled, shoving a thick forefinger at Ki. "Don't you hear so good or what? Look at this yeller bugger, Fred. He's just sittin' here like he owns the whole damn railroad."

"Kick his ass off the train is what we oughta do," the one named Fred grated. "Maybe if he has to walk the next fifty miles to Cheyenne he'll remember his manners."

"Yeah, by gawd! Let's throw him off the train and be done with it!"

The man clamped his big hand on Ki's arm, and only then did the samurai look up to meet his eyes.

"Let go of me," Ki said quietly. "Or I will break your wrist."

The big laborer in his bib overalls was so stunned that he actually did release Ki for a moment. He pulled his hand back and stared. He outweighed Ki by at least sixty pounds, and most of it was muscle earned loading trains and wagons.

Then he grinned at his partner. "Did you hear that, Fred? By dammed, he's a fiesty little slant-eye, ain't he?"

"Earl, beat the livin' hell out of him," Fred hissed.

Ki studied the two men. If anything, Fred was the more imposing. He stood well over six feet tall and had a scarred fighter's face with the traditional fist-busted nose.

A hard-looking group of men came into the coach at that minute. There were six of them, and something in their faces told Ki they were dead serious about whatever it was they intended to do.

For a minute, he thought they were lawmen, but when they passed, he saw no sign of a badge. Their sudden appearance stopped all conversation in the coach, and they were so dangerous looking that even Earl and Fred forgot their sport until the six passed and slammed the door behind them.

"They looked tetchy as a pit full of teased snakes," Earl said.

"Sure did. But what about the chink here? I'm tired of standing and he needs a good long hike."

Earl nodded. He grabbed Ki by the arm and started to yank him out of the seat.

The rock-hard edge of Ki's hand chopped down on Earl's wrist in a *tegatana* blow. There was a cry of pain, and then Earl's face went pale as he grabbed his wrist and bellowed. "He broke the sonofabitch, Fred! Kill him!"

Fred's massive fist blurred in a short punch that Ki could not avoid because he was pinned in the seat.

He took the blow on the side of his face, and as Fred reached back with his left hand knotted in a fist, Ki threw his weight backward and then used a vicious snap-kick that connected with Fred's crotch. The big man howled. He was doubled up in pain and Ki smashed him across the cheek, opening it to the bone.

Through tears of pain, Earl went for his gun and had it halfway up when Ki grabbed his thumb and bent it backward until he drove him to his knees. The gun clattered harmlessly to the coach's floor, and then Ki's hand whipped upward in a *migi-shotei* blow that caught his opponent just below his jaw. Earl's eyes bugged. His face went pale and he collapsed between the seats gagging for breath.

His body trapped, Ki struggled to break free. Fred sledged him with a thundering overhand blow that sent the samurai crashing over his bench seat. Before Ki could shake the cobwebs out of his head, the man kicked him in the side of the ribs. Ki barely had time to throw his weight with the force of the kick, and avoid having his ribs caved in.

40

"Get up, you yellow bastard!" Fred yelled, his face flushed with pain, one hand still hanging down to protect his aching crotch. "I'm going to break your neck!"

Ki rose to his feet. His hands were up, left extended out a little, right pulled back close to his chest, fingers bent so that the knuckles were straight and ready to inflict maximum damage. He was in a semi-crouch as he waited for the bigger man to attack.

He did not have to wait long.

Fred lunged forward, his face cruel and confident. He drove an uppercut from somewhere around his knees. The man was fast. Ki stepped back, feeling the smoky air move, and then his own fist drove forward in a perfectly timed, perfectly executed punch that sent Fred slamming sideways into the seats. The old Indian woman kept chanting and men grabbed Fred and shoved him forward.

Fred wiped his face and said, "The hell with this!" His hand streaked for his gun.

Ki waited until the weapon was out of the holster. Then he sent a sweep kick upward that connected with the six-gun and sent it spinning through an open window.

"Why you—"

Whatever he was about to say was cut short as Ki attacked with two punishing strikes to the face that sent Fred reeling backward. When the powerful man was grabbed and thrown forward once more, Ki simply stopped him dead in his tracks with a foot-strike to the stomach that bent him like a rusty nail and left him gasping like a beached fish, unable to breathe.

Ki stepped forward, his eyes on the exposed back of Fred's neck. He could have broken it with ease, or simply knocked Fred unconscious. But he did neither. A samurai did not gloat in victory or compromise his honor by strik-

41

ing an already beaten opponent—especially an unworthy one.

Ki turned away. Just as he did, a dull explosion rocked the train.

"What the hell was that?" someone yelled.

Ki knew. Knew that the men who had passed through the coach a short time before had blown open the vault that held eighty thousand dollars plus Jessica Starbuck's five thousand. He leaped for the rear door, his eyes on the mail coach and the open door banging in the wind.

He saw the outlaws standing in the smoky car, and when one of them fired at him, Ki threw himself sideways, almost going over the side.

Two more shots drove him back into the third-class coach, and as he reached for one of the many *shuriken* star-blades hidden in his vest, Fred stepped up behind him and brought the barrel of a shotgun down across the back of Ki's head.

The samurai collapsed in the aisle.

"Did you feel or hear something back in the train?" Jessie asked suddenly.

"Why, no," William Lamar said. He had been telling her all about his youth in Denver, which Jessie was surprised to find moderately interesting. Actually, the young attorney was quite an amusing storyteller when he relaxed a little bit.

Jessie stood up. "Will you excuse me for a few minutes? I think I'll go back and investigate—just in case."

"Let me go instead."

"No," she said. "I'm sure it's nothing and I want to see how Ki is getting along. Besides, I'd appreciate it if you'd watch my briefcase."

42

He looked very disappointed but Jessie was quite firm, so he remained seated.

"I'll be right back and you can finish telling me that story about the time your uncle was chased by the circus bear."

He brightened. "That's one of my favorites."

Jessie hurried down the aisle. On the range, she wore a specially made Colt revolver that her father had gotten at the Colt factory in Connecticut. The gun had been designed especially for Jessie. It was considerably lighter than the popular Colt .45, and was chambered to take a .38 caliber bullet. Jessie could draw and fire the gun as swiftly and accurately as all but the very best gunmen—the so-called professionals.

But now, her sixgun was packed away in her luggage and all she carried was a single-shot derringer that was hidden in a fold of her dress.

She passed through four cars and each seemed oblivious to the commotion that had set her alarm bells to ringing. Maybe she was being unreasonable in her worry, but it was her experience that instincts seldom failed if you listened to them carefully.

Jessie passed through one coach, and just as she prepared to enter another, a man stepped in behind her and shoved a gun in her spine. "I'd just bet anything that you'd be the rich and beautiful Miss Jessica Starbuck. Just the woman I was told to invite to our little party."

Jessie froze. They were on the swaying platform between two coaches. Jessie turned slowly and made herself smile. The outlaw with the gun smiled too.

"Damn, you're pretty," he said.

Jessie's hand moved into the pocket of her dress as her

eyes locked with his. "Thank you," she said, pulling out her derringer and firing it down at his foot.

The man screeched in pain, and when he reached for his boot and began to hop around on one leg, Jessie snatched his sixgun and then shoved him hard.

He hollered as his body was sent spinning out into space. She saw him strike the side of the roadbed and go somersaulting down onto the prairie, where he lay still.

Jessie took a moment to check his gun. Then she headed into the third-class coach.

"Look out!" someone yelled from the floor as an outlaw's gun exploded at the far end of the coach.

Jessie threw herself back outside and grabbed the rail of the platform as two more bullets came crashing through the glass-windowed door. She took a deep breath. Where was Ki? Had they killed him and thrown him off the train? Or perhaps they'd taken him hostage, although that did not seem very likely.

"Miss Starbuck, can you hear me?"

"Yes!" she yelled.

"We got your Oriental friend back in the baggage car. You come on back with your hands up or we kill him. What's it going to be?"

Jessie swore silently. Her shoulders sagged and she said, "I'll come. Don't kill him."

Cold laughter floated down through the dirty railroad car. "Get your pretty tail back here in a hurry. We got some negotiating to do."

Jessie stepped back into the car and started down the aisle with her hands up. On both sides of her everyone except the chanting squaw lay spread-eagled. Another outlaw had them all covered with a sawed-off shotgun.

The man with the gun was leering with triumph. "We

44

figured eighty thousand dollars was plenty of reason enough to take this train. But as it turns out, you might be worth even more than the whole railroad itself! We are sure running in the luck today!"

"Where's Ki?" she asked tightly.

"In the baggage car. Knocked out colder than cellar-stored cider."

"What are you going to do with us?"

He shoved her into the baggage car. There were three dead lawmen piled up along one wall. The broken door of the safe was still smoking. "My friends," the outlaw said, "I want you to meet one of the richest women in the whole wide world! Miss Jessica Starbuck!"

The outlaws grinned. They had been counting the money and Jessie saw that her own leather case was now empty. "Where is Ki?" she demanded.

"Over there. Other than the fact he has decided to take a long sleep, he's right as rain, Miss Starbuck."

Jessie started for him, and when a man blocked her path, she hissed, "Get out of my way!"

The leader nodded. Jessie knelt beside the samurai. He appeared to be knocked out cold. She reached up and examined his scalp and found it caked with blood. But with her hand on his, she felt him move and she knew a breath of hope.

"You've almost killed him," she swore, turning to face them. "His scalp is split wide open!"

"He's alive, ain't he? And he and you will both stay that way if you cooperate and do as you're told."

"What do you want?"

"We want you to accompany a couple of us right up to the head of the train. We climb over the coal tender and order the engineer to stop a few miles up ahead where we have horses waiting. Then we take a little ride."

"And Ki? What happens to him?"

"He goes right on sleeping peaceably," the outlaw said as he stepped forward and grabbed Jessie's arm. "Boys, you be ready to unload when the train stops."

"What about all the passengers up in the coaches?" a man asked. "They're carrying money and gold."

"Don't be greedy," the leader snapped. "We take Miss Starbuck for a ride and the best is yet to come."

They laughed at that—laughed long and hard as Jessie was shoved forward.

The outlaws were in control. As Jessie and the man behind her passed through each coach, she saw that they had a man stationed at each end with a shotgun at the ready. Everyone was on the floors.

When they passed into the first-class coach, Jessie saw William Lamar on the floor like all the others. He looked stricken with fright but Jessie gave him a tight smile and his face changed. And suddenly, without warning, he jumped up from the floor with a gun in his fist and opened fire.

Women screamed. Men cussed and the outlaws dove for the rear door. Lamar was no gunman, but then it was close work. A wild bullet caught the outlaw leader in the calf, and when he tried to grab Jessie and use her as a shield, she knocked the gun out of his hand.

"Freeze!" William Lamar screamed. "Even I can't keep missing at this range!"

And to make sure, he ran right up to the outlaw leader and shoved the gun to his skull. "Don't make me blow what little brains you have out!"

Jessie picked up the outlaw's gun. She could not believe

that Lamar had found enough courage to do such a thing. But he had, and she was filled with gratitude.

"Someone go tell the locomotive engineer to stop the train right now—before we reach the rest of the gang and their waiting horses. In the meantime, everyone get up and follow me back to the mail car. We're going to clean out this bunch!"

Men jumped off the floor and found their weapons. Jessie and Lamar headed for the doorway.

They opened fire into the next coach and the outlaws began a retreat. And by the time they reached the third-class coach, the entire train was packed with furious passengers plenty ready to fight.

"Listen, everyone," Jessie yelled. "We have got to take them from both ends. When you hear me come in from the caboose, open fire!" Jessie grabbed the wooden ladder and began to climb onto the roof.

"My God!" Lamar cried. "You're going to go up there?"

"I sure am. Coming?"

The attorney swallowed noisily, but he came up and showed his true colors. There was a rail walkway that the brakemen used to traverse the line of coaches and brake the train on steep downgrades.

"Did you bring that gun?" she asked, glancing around to see him swaying precariously.

"Yes," he cried, staring down at the racing countryside.

"Don't look down! Did you reload the gun?"

He shook his head and she said, "Why don't we stop and reload?"

He nodded and dropped to the platform, then looked up at her and said, "I don't have any extra bullets!"

Jessie shook her head. "Never mind. Come on. Let's get this over with."

With sure steps, she hurried across the coach until she came to the caboose. Maybe, she reasoned, it was better that William was out of bullets. He'd almost shot her by mistake back in the coach, but there was one thing she would never forget—when the chips were down, William Lamar had showed real courage and heart.

Jessie was proud of him.

Chapter 5

Jessie eased down the ladder between the caboose and the mail car full of train robbers. The besieged gang below were not expecting anyone to traverse the roof of a moving train. When she reached the swaying platform, she could see them all up toward the front of the mail car, waiting for an attack.

William missed a ladder and went flying out over the roadbed. His shoes clattered loudly against the side of the coach, and Jessie had to holster her gun and make a wild grab to rescue him. Somehow, she pulled him back onto the platform and they found themselves hugging each other.

"You all right?" she whispered, knowing her words could not be heard over the banging of the iron wheels and track underneath them.

He nodded. Did not seem to want to let go of her. Jessie had to pry his long arms from around her body.

"You stay back here out of sight."

"But—"

"Don't argue!" she said. "Your gun is empty and there is no sense in getting killed for nothing."

She turned to enter the mail coach. She counted eight men. There was no way in the world she could kill or wound them all. But she could see Ki slowly coming to his feet. Maybe, if they were very, very lucky...

Suddenly, William lunged in front of her and snatched the gun out of her fist. "Freeze!" he screamed, pushing Jessie behind him to shield her from danger.

The outlaws swung around and William opened fire. His gun bucked again and again and bullets screamed into wood, through canvas mailbags, off the blown vault door, and especially through the open door around them. William took a bullet in the upper arm that spun him halfway around. Jessie heard William's gun click on an empty cylinder. She grabbed him and they fell over backward in a hail of lead. The mail coach was filled with gunsmoke. Back in the third-class coach the other passengers opened fire.

"Stay down!" Jessie yelled, hugging William close as bullets continued to whip-crack over their heads. They began to inch out of the doorway, which was being splintered to kindling wood.

William and Jessie rolled out onto the platform and managed to climb back up the ladder. A moment later, they were on the roof of the mail car again and they could feel the train beginning to slow.

"If they come up here after us, we can't even defend ourselves, Miss Starbuck! Not without any bullets."

"They won't come," Jessie said, "because they've got a whole trainload of angry passengers ahead of them—and Ki right behind."

William blinked. He watched as Jessie ripped a piece of her clothing to make a quick bandage for his wounded arm. "You're the bravest, most beautiful woman I've ever seen

50

in my life," he said unabashedly. "I worship you. I'd give my life to save yours."

Jessie was a woman who heard compliments from men almost daily. But when those compliments were given with such unreserved honesty, she felt a little humbled. Finishing the bandage job, she looked into his round eyes. "You are a very, very brave man, William. Maybe a little foolish, but that can certainly be forgiven in light of what you tried to do to save my life."

"I'd do it all over again. Honest. I'd do . . . anything for you."

She kissed him on the mouth—hard and quick. He almost became paralyzed.

"Why . . . ?"

"Because I wanted to. And because a woman doesn't find a knight very often. But most of all, because I don't wish to be placed on a pedestal."

"But you're rich and beautiful, brave and—"

She kissed him once more. "And a woman. No more. No less."

Jessie looked away. As the train shuddered to a halt, outlaws began to come flying off, but they were immediately shot as passengers unloaded to give them chase. Without horses waiting, it was no contest. The train had at least a hundred men capable of fighting. The outlaws were down to less than a half-dozen.

"Look!" Jessie said pointing down below, "There's Ki!"

The samurai had come flying off the train in a low dive that brought him down on two running outlaws. He drove them to the earth, and, as they tried to raise their sixguns, Ki's hands and feet struck with stunning efficiency. It took the samurai less than ten seconds to disable both men.

"Look out!" Jessie yelled helplessly, as another outlaw

came tumbling off the train, raised his gun, and took aim. Jessie hurled an empty Colt at the man but it was a wasted effort.

Ki dropped to his knees as a bullet went over his head. His hand found one of the deadly *shuriken* blades, and Jessie saw it glint in the sun as it traveled straight to the outlaw's chest. The man cried out and dropped his sixgun. He grabbed his chest and then pitched over and rolled down the embankment to lie still on the prairie.

Jessie and William watched as the last two outlaws surrendered and begged for mercy.

"It's over," she said, waving down to Ki.

The samurai, caked blood on the side of his handsome face, waved back.

Jessie stood up. "Come on, William, let's get off this thing and get our feet on solid ground."

He nodded eagerly. "I always thought I was afraid of heights, Miss Starbuck. And now that I've again the time to think about it, I guess I still am."

"Well," she said, "we are all afraid of some things in life. But it takes a good man to know his fears and still overcome them in an emergency."

William stared down at the earth from what did seem like a dizzying height. "Yeah, but what if, when the emergency is over, all the old fears come rushing right back?"

"Then you know you're just human, William," Jessie said. As she studied this thin, slightly myopic, and very unusual attorney, Jessie was reminded once again that real heroes came in all colors, shapes, and sizes. Ki was a hero today as he was every day of his life. And if he had not been down in that mail car, the outlaws would have come flooding out the back door and most surely have climbed the ladder to shoot them off the roof.

But for a man like William Lamar to show such unexpected courage—now that was even more special. Jessie would not underestimate this new attorney of hers again.

In Cheyenne, the four train robbers who had survived were handed over to the authorities, and, maybe, because he was such an unlikely-looking hero, William Lamar got most of the crowd's attention.

The town feted all three of them for saving the sale money. They had a little parade in which Jessie, Ki and William rode up and down the street while people clapped and a few overexuberant cowboys even shot off their guns.

"Look!" Jessie said to her attorney, pointing to a pair of pretty young ladies who were waving silk handkerchiefs and yelling William's name amidst all the commotion. "You've got a bunch of fans here already."

But William shook his head. "No, ma'am. After being in your sunlight, all other women seem pale and like nothing."

Jessie frowned with disappointment. She wondered if William had ever been with a woman. She suspected he had not.

"How old are you?"

"Twenty-two," he said.

"You should go make their acquaintance," Jessie urged.

"Nope. I got too much to think about in Skull Creek. No time for girls. I want to find a lawyer here in Cheyenne and get him to loan or sell me some more law books."

"You won't have long to study them. The train pulls out tomorrow morning."

"I know that. But I don't intend to sleep any until the trial is over. I'm going to win the case for you no matter what it takes."

Jessie shook her head. She didn't doubt for a moment that William Lamar was sincere. But he certainly seemed to be confusing his devotion to her with the true purpose of his job—to win the freedom of two falsely accused sheepmen.

I'll have to make him find a way to understand that he is doing this for Pete Bodie and his son, not for me, Jessie thought.

The wagon came to a stop beside a reviewing stand, and the mayor of Cheyenne gave a rousing speech about courage. The speech was good for the first quarter-hour, and then the man started repeating himself.

Finally, as the sun began to set, Jessie stood up and walked over to the podium and said, "We did what was necessary and, while I understand that we saved the ranch-sale money, I also had a significant sum in that vault that I did not want to lose. But I wanted to say that my friends, Ki and William . . . William?"

She saw him walking away from the crowd.

"He's gone to find an attorney and get those law books," Ki said with a faint shrug of his shoulders.

Jessie turned back to the crowd. "William Lamar of Denver," she continued, "are the real heroes. And now, because it has been a long, trying day, I ask that you excuse us. I thank you for your generous praise."

As the crowd dispersed, a big man in his sixties wearing expensive clothes and a huge diamond ring came up to Jessie. "Miss Starbuck, my name is Bob Hammer and I am the man whose eighty thousand dollars you saved today. I'd like to thank you personally by taking you and your friends out to dinner tonight."

"No, thank you," Jessie said, after glancing at Ki. "We have an early-morning train to catch."

54

"Where are you going?"

"Skull Creek."

"Mighty rough sort of a town." The cattleman frowned. "I know this is not the time or the place, but I wanted to ask you about that young fella, William Lamar from Denver."

"What about him?"

"Well, I had a chance to talk to several people, and it seems he is quite a fella. I'd like to hire him away from you, Miss Starbuck. But I am not a man to do something behind the back of a beautiful woman who helped save me a pile of money."

"Mr. Lamar is free to work for you if you present him with a better offer," Jessie said.

"I already did that. I told him that I'd pay double whatever you are paying. Know what he said?"

Jessie shook her head.

"He said no amount of money in the world could buy him away from you. I think that young man is in for a pretty rough surprise when he learns that you are famous for being all business."

"I see." Jessie thanked the cattleman and left him, feeling more than a little troubled.

It was long after midnight when she arose from her bed and pulled on her dressing gown. Jessie left her room and walked two doors down the dimly lit hallway. Light flowed out from under ·William Lamar's door. Jessie knocked softly.

"Who is it? Go away!"

Jessie knocked again and this time William's voice was close. "I said—"

"It's me, Jessie Starbuck. May I have a word with you?"

"Oh, sure!"

He unbolted the door and let her in. He was still dressed but his bed was rumpled and covered with law books. And in the pale light of his bedside lamp, he looked dead tired and suddenly very nervous.

"William," she began, "we need to talk about something important."

His eager grin failed him completely. "All right."

"I want you to relax a little bit. And promise not to risk your life for me again. You've proved your loyalty, but I don't want you getting killed for it."

"But I *had* to do it for you."

"I think," Jessie said slowly, as she moved over to the bed and sat down, "that perhaps you should have taken that better job offer."

"No! I could *never* leave you and—"

Jessie patted the bed and he came obediently over to her side. "Sit down," she ordered, pushing his books and notes aside and patting the bedspread.

He sat.

"William, I admire your courage, your loyalty, and your dedication. But I can't abide a man who acts like a slave, or like a puppy waiting for its master's call."

He gulped, removed his glasses, and stared at her. "I do that?"

"Yes." She reached over and turned off the light. "And I know now that I'll have to do something rather unusual to take care of this problem—to make you act like a man instead of a faithful pet."

Jessie reached for him.

"Ouch!" he said. "My arm."

"Sorry," Jessie said, pushing him down on the bed and unbuttoning his collar.

"What are you doing?"

"For the very short time we have left before morning, I'm going to make us equal, like partners," she said as she unbuttoned his shirt and ran her fingers over his chest. "And when daylight streams through the window, you are either going to treat me like a woman and a friend, or I'm going to insist you take that other job. I need someone who is not afraid to act on his own to openly question my judgement if he feels it is important. I pay people to think and act, not to jump on my string." She unbuckled his pants, slid her hand down until she found his long, soft male member. "I was trained as a *geisha*. Do you know what that means."

He gulped and managed to whisper "No."

"Then I'll show you."

"But I . . ."

Whatever he was about to say was instantly forgotten as Jessie pulled her nightgown away to reveal her lush, perfectly formed breasts, which she lowered gently to his face.

As instinctively as a baby, he took one in his mouth and moaned with happiness as Jessie stroked his manhood into a towering erection.

His hands reached around and gripped her buttocks and then slipped between her legs. He had long, delicate fingers, and used them to probe the golden mass of hair until he dipped into her honeyed wetness.

Jessie sighed with pleasure as her hips began to rock back and forth over him. "Maybe you're not quite the innocent virgin that I imagined you to be."

He laughed softly. "I'm no virgin, but neither have I ever even dreamed of making love to a woman like you."

Jessie's legs parted wide, for he was long and thick. She placed the tip of his big erection into herself with a contented sigh. "Dreams come true, William, but I can tell you this much. You'll give as good as you get tonight."

To prove it, she hunched down, suddenly driving his throbbing rod up into her. It felt wonderful! And when he began to pump energetically, Jessie came down hard on him and smothered his exertions.

"Go slow, William," she breathed, feeling his hands cup her firm buttocks. "Make this last."

He tried to still his body, but it seemed to behave with a mind of its own. Jessie could feel him trembling, and then her own body began to jerk faster. But when she sensed that he was almost ready to explode, she stopped and lifted herself up until only a little of him entered her.

"Oh," he breathed, "I've died and am standing at the gates of heaven. Don't close them!"

"Not yet," she told him. Jessie held herself suspended over his body, then, ever so slowly, her lovely hips began to rotate once more. She used the muscles of her vagina to coax and milk every last nerve ending in his body of its ultimate pleasure. He was breathing fast but so was she.

"Please," he begged, his thighs straining upward, "I can't stand this another second!"

But Jessie shook her head. She watched his face in the starlight that entered his open window. Her motion quickened and she found she was having trouble maintaining her own control as his lean hips began to make frantic jerking motions that were driving her wild with desire.

Then, suddenly, a low growl of pleasure erupted from

his throat. No longer able to control himself, he dug his fingers into her buttocks and began to buck and ram himself deep into her.

"No more!" he cried, rolling her over onto his legal notes. Now on top and wild with desire, he began driving himself in and out of her with deep, plunging strokes.

Jessie laughed softly. He had taken control! She wrapped her long legs around his hips and whispered, "Come on, Bill, take me like a man!"

He did. With a roar of pleasure, he buried his staff to the hilt in her hot juices, and when he exploded, he filled her completely.

They lay spent, bodies bathed in perspiration, breath still coming fast, every limb drained and relaxed.

"Jessie," he said.

She turned to study his face. "Yes?"

"I never like being called William. I want you to call me Bill."

"All right."

"Will you ever let me make love to you again?"

"I don't know," she answered truthfully. "I don't think you'll ever act like a puppy again."

He chuckled, rolled over, and began to kiss her breasts until she writhed with pleasure. "In that case," he said, "I'm going to make the most of every moment we have."

Jessie smiled in the semi-darkness and opened herself wide for him. Somehow, she knew that the boy who had left Denver had become a man—on the train, and here in this bed. And maybe that would be the difference between winning the lives of the Bodies, father and son.

It was something that bore thinking about, but as he

drove himself strongly in and out of her eager womanhood, thoughts evaporated like mist in sunlight. And Jessie bit her lip as pleasure carried her toward another thundering climax.

Chapter 6

They left Cheyenne on the Union Pacific, and when they had crossed almost the entire breadth of Wyoming, they came to Rock Springs. Jessie bought horses, saddles, and supplies, and they rode north up the long slope of the Continental Divide. The country was dry, the soil pale and powdery, the sagebrush bleached-looking and stunted.

This was a hard land where the winters lasted five months and summers were scorching hot. Jessie studied the land with an experienced eye and decided it was damn poor cattle country. Not enough water, not enough graze. It would take about a hundred acres for every longhorn cow, and that meant lean profits for any cattleman.

But it was good sheep country. The small, stunted clumps of grass, the brush and sage, were exactly the kind of graze that sheep could flourish upon.

South Pass City was a roaring cattle and mining town laid right up near the top of the Continental Divide and providentially set in a canyon, where it would escape the icy winters that swept across the summits of these Wind River Mountains.

They spent the night in nearby Atlantic City and had

trouble sleeping because of the huge ore-stamping mills. Miners jammed the saloons and sang boisterous, drunken songs until daybreak. An occasional gunshot punctuated the music and laughter. Eager to be on their way, they rode out very early and soon began to descend into the Wind River country. With each mile the air grew hotter, but they could see that great valley stretched out below and, as far as the eye could reach, they noted the massive cattle ranches.

"Now that," Jessie said, easing down from her horse to admire the vista, "is cattle country." She could track the broad, meandering Wind River as it lazily churned northeast toward distant, gray-green mountains.

"Where is Skull Creek?" Bill asked.

Jessie pointed northeast to where the land grew hard again and the sagebrush clotted the landscape and crouched at the valley's edge. "Somewhere beyond those hills, according to the map I was given by the man who sold me these horses."

"I wonder why would they put a town way out there with this green valley so close?" Ki asked.

"I don't know." Jessie checked her cinch, found it loose, and tightened it before she remounted. "But I suppose it's the same story as anywhere else in the West. The first cattlemen in this valley claimed all the bottom land, the grass, and the river. Later, more cattlemen came and they took up ranches along the edges of the valley. And finally, a few without good sense actually carved out some of that high desert land. It's probably a living, but not much more."

She touched spurs to her horse and they rode on down into the valley. The ranches she could see were all prosperous looking. Cattle grazed in knee-high grass along the

Wind River, and she saw irrigation ditches carrying water to hundreds of acres of green pasture land.

A barefoot boy on an old swayback horse came galloping out to greet them. He could not have been more than thirteen, sunburned and freckled. "You want to buy some fresh apples or apricots?" he asked eagerly.

"Sure," Jessie said. She pulled a dollar out of her jeans and watched the boy unbutton his sagging shirt and unload a half-dozen each of his home-grown treasures. The apples were small and green—not a great deal larger than eggs—but the apricots looked delicious.

"I ain't got but twenty-five cents' worth, ma'am."

"Take the dollar and tell me exactly where Skull Creek is located."

The boy pointed between his horse's ears and said, "About twenty miles out thataway. But was I you, I'd stay here in Lander or even over in Riverton, ma'am."

"Why is that?"

"Skull Creek is a hard town to live in, an easy one to die in. My pa, he won't even allow me to go over there— ever. They're fixin' to hang a man next week, though."

Jessie glanced quickly over at Bill, who said, "Have they already had the trial?"

The boy just shrugged. "Don't know about no trial or anything. They're gonna hang a sheepman named Pete Bodie. He's got a son. Growed man that they want to hang, too. He's bein' damned hard to catch though. Stays out in these hills and in those mountains you come offa. I seen him a time or two. He carries a Winchester and a big old buffalo rifle that he can blow the eye out of a bird with at a mile distant."

Jessie knew that was quite an exaggeration. "Do you know where he is most of the time?"

"Nope," the boy said. "And neither does anyone else. He moves, all the time, he moves around. They hunt him like a dog but he keeps 'em back with that big rifle. There ain't no man that can outshoot him. They're afraid to get within range 'cause they know he'll kill the first man."

Jessie looked up at the mountains. "Is there any way to leave him a message?"

"Don't seem possible, ma'am. He'd waved at me a time or two, maybe 'cause I'm a boy. He and his pa killed Elvin Pattison, though. And they're gonna hang for it sure. Just like all the other murderin' sheepmen."

The boy shook his head wistfully. "I sure wisht I could ride this horse over there to see the hangin'. But my ma and pa, they're all-fired het up agin' it. Say a hangin' is a dirty and mean thing to watch."

"They're right," Jessie said. "It is."

The boy pulled his hat off and scratched his head. "If'n that's so, then why does everybody from this valley ride over and see them Skull Creek folks every time they hang another sheepman?"

Jessie's expression became bleak. "I never could figure out what people saw in watching another human being hung." She looked at the boy. "Your mother and father, they sound like they're more sensible than most people in this valley. You listen to them well, and learn."

"You really gonna let me keep this whole dollar?"

"I really am," Jessie whispered, taking the apricots and sharing them with Ki and Bill. When she bit into one, it was as tasty as she had hoped.

Noting her appreciation, the boy smiled and said, "The apricots are the best. To be real truthful, ma'am, you might want to give them apples to your horses. They're a little on the bitter side."

She nodded. "We'll do that."

They rode off then and pushed the horses into a gallop. It was good to know that Pete Bodie was still alive, but it seemed to be a foregone conclusion that he would hang.

They found the road into Skull Creek and discovered it to be in a huge valley, some twenty miles long and almost as wide. Down the valley's length ran Skull Creek, little more than a trickle of water in summer. As in Wind River, there were big cattle ranches here, but to a rancher like Jessie, the observable difference was as obvious as night and day.

Skull Creek ranches had a worn-down-at-the-heels look to them. The houses and outbuildings were splintered and gray from age and no paint. The fences were two- and even one-strand barbed wire affairs supported by branches and sticks instead of the good cedar posts that were used on her own Circle Star ranch down in Texas. The land itself was powder-dry, best suited for horned toads, lizards, and long-eared jackrabbits. The few cattle Jessie saw were already thin and pinched up in the flanks. And they'd get thinner as the hot summer wore on into fall.

"Look up to the north toward the head of the valley," Ki said, pointing into the distance.

"I see." Jessie replied.

"What do you see?" Bill Lamar asked, shading his eyes with his hand because he had not yet bought a decent Stetson hat.

Jessie explained. "Up there at the head of the valley, you can tell that the grass is greener. What has obviously happened is that the ranchers who first spilled over into this valley claimed the headwater and dammed up the stream, leaving nothing more than a trickle of water for their downstream neighbors."

"They can do that?"

"You bet they can. Happens all the time. They've got first claim on the water rights. In the winter, fall, and especially in the early spring, it doesn't matter much because there is enough water for everyone. But later on, it gets critical. And since cows and horses drink year around, you need to determine the carrying capacity of your range by the time of year when it is at its worst. That's usually July, August, and September."

"Doesn't sound very fair to me," Bill said. "But I don't know anything about water rights."

"You'd better start to learn after this trial is over. In the West, water is life. Whoever controls it can turn desert land into pasture."

Bill nodded. "It makes sense. That must be Skull Creek up ahead. Don't look like much, does it?"

Jessie shook her head. Skull Creek was a main street about a quarter-mile long. On each side of it were two or three blocks of shacks and a few painted houses with shade trees. Four tall windmills turned listlessly, cranking up the precious underground water for drinking, now that the creek was so low and undoubtedly fouled by cattle when it reached the town.

Skull Creek looked as grim as its name.

They rode in and stabled their horses at the only place in town. Jessie missed Sun, but it would not have been practical to freight him all the way to Rock Springs just for a hundred-mile ride.

"Where is the sheriff's office?" she asked the old stablemaster whose stalls were filthy, and whose corrals were so pathetic she doubted they could have contained milk cows, let alone horses.

"Up the street yonder," the man said. "You come to see Pete Bodie dance at the end of a rope?"

"We came to see that he doesn't hang at all," Bill Lamar said, his eyes narrowing to slits behind his glasses.

"Then you might as well ride on out of here. The trial starts tomorrow and it'll end tomorrow. They may even *hang* old Pete tomorrow, but they'll probably make him sweat it out a few days first."

"The hell they will!" Bill said. "Where is he?"

"Jail."

"Where's that?"

The liveryman blinked. "The same place the sheriff's office is, o'course! Who are you, anyway?"

Ki said, "You'll find out tomorrow, oldtimer."

They left with their saddlebags stuffed with money and personal belongings. Ordinarily, they'd have stopped at one of the two sorry looking little hotels first. But they'd come too far too fast to put off the confrontation a minute longer.

"Don't expect a welcome," Jessie warned Bill. "It's both Ki's and my own experience that the last thing people like is to have outsiders come in and change the plan of things. These people seem to expect a fast trail and a hanging. They're not going to be pleased if we change that."

"If Pete Bodie is innocent and the judge is honest, I'll get him off," Bill vowed.

"I know you'll try. But if the judge is crooked, I'll have to find a way to get him off the bench."

"How?"

"I don't have any idea," Jessie admitted. "Let's just hope it doesn't come to that point."

The sheriff's office was a rathole, crammed with old boxes, garbage yet to be tossed into the alley, and various parts of saddles in stages of repair. When they walked in, the sheriff was sitting hunched over his desk stitching up the cantle of a saddle. He was a big man, but one gone to lard. He wore a two-day growth of gray beard, a battered hat, a dirty white shirt, and ugly red suspenders to hold his pants up and directly under his nail-keg-sized belly. Jessie saw him look up and then back down at his saddle. He was quite obviously not a sociable man, and one who had to supplement his meager sheriff's salary with his leatherwork.

"Hello there," she said, looking at the only cell in the office and seeing the once familiar face of Pete Bodie, who was snoring as peacefully as a child on his thin straw mattress.

"What do you want?" the sheriff asked without looking up again.

"We want to talk to your prisoner."

Now the sheriff looked up. "What for?"

"We think he might be innocent."

"He ain't."

Bill said, "Is he being represented by a competent attorney at law?"

"You mean has he got his own lawyer?"

"That's right."

"Nope," the sheriff said. "There's only one in town, and he's the one that is prosecuting him."

"Then I intend to represent him," Bill said, stepping toward the jail cell.

The sheriff was surprisingly fast for a man as fat as he was. He came out of his chair in a rush, grabbed Bill by the collar, and yanked him around. He must have weighed a hundred pounds more than Bill, and he shook the much younger man like a terrier would a stick.

68

"You, the Chinaman, and your pretty girlfriend get the hell outta here and let me do my work."

Ki stepped over. "Let go of him," he said quietly.

The sheriff shoved Bill so hard he crashed up against the wall. "Chinaman," he hissed, "we tar and feather you yellow bastards and send you out with a rail tied between your legs."

Ki's face stiffened. "I'm not Chinese," he said, "and if you ever insult me again like that, I'll make you regret it."

The sheriff flushed with anger, and before he could take a swing at Ki and get hurt, Jessie stepped in between them and said. "My name is Jessica Starbuck. This is Ki. He is half Japanese and half white. The young man you just shook is qualified to practice law and represent your prisoner tomorrow in court. And if you haven't understood what I've just said, then I suggest you go find the judge and get him over here very quickly before you make any more serious and dangerous mistakes."

The sheriff stepped back. "I don't take kindly to being told what to do, Jessica Starbuck. I heard of you when I was a sheriff down in New Mexico. Your pa, he was pretty big stuff, but he got took down to size. You and these two hirelings of yours mess around here, you'll get took down to size the same way."

Ki's hands streaked out, and he slapped the lawman across the mouth. "Don't ever threaten her life again," he whispered.

The man roared and jumped at Ki, and the samurai sent a flat-foot kick straight into that big belly. The sheriff groaned. His cheeks puffed out and he staggered. Ki moved in and kicked him in the buttocks and he went crashing into the jail cell so hard that Pete Bodie was jarred out of his nap.

69

The sheriff clawed for his gun, but Jessie had anticipated that and she had her own gun out and pointed at his head. "Don't do it, Sheriff."

The lawman was no fool. He shoved his gun back into his holster and spat. "Miss Starbuck, you may be a big deal in Texas, but this is Wyoming and you're nothing! You'll be sorry you ever came to Skull Creek. Both of you."

He pointed a shaking finger at Bill. "Lawyer, you better start thinking of a way to save these two instead of Pete. He's already a dead man and this pair is pushing for the same damn end."

"Go find the judge," Jessie ordered in a cold, flat tone of voice. "I think we have said all we need to say."

The sheriff grabbed a double-barreled shotgun from his gunrack. He broke it and stuffed in two shells. "If you try to bust him outta my jail, I'll be waiting outside. And there's nothing I'd rather do than nail all three of you!"

When the man slammed the shotgun together and stomped out the door to find the judge, Jessie turned to face Pete Bodie.

He was on his feet, much smaller and much older than she had imagined. He looked tired, beaten, and almost fragile. But the moment he smiled and she saw the spark in his eyes, she knew that she was wrong. Those twinkling eyes might be a little pale and a little rheumy-looking, but they were the eyes of a fighter. A man who would never give up on life.

"So," he said, "God sent an angel all the way up from Texas and her name is Jessica Starbuck."

Despite the grim circumstances, Jessie had to laugh. "Only the second part is true. I'm no angel, but I am a Texan and Alex's daughter."

"How'd you know about me and this mess I got catched up in?"

Jessie showed him the letter she had received from his son. He read it twice, very slowly, his lips moving over every word. "So," he said finally, "I should have guessed it was Mike. He always remembered you, even though you were just kids the last time we visited your father's ranch. You must have made quite an impression."

"Pete, before the sheriff comes storming back in here, why don't you tell us all you can about this trouble. Bill here is going to represent you in court tomorrow, and my friend Ki will see that you are protected."

Pete shook hands with them both, but it was Ki he was most interested in. "I can see that you are an Oriental and, knowing how highly Alex Starbuck regarded the samurai, I'd bet anything you are one of them."

"You'd be right," Ki said, showing pleasure at this compliment.

"Tell us exactly what happened," Bill urged, his voice anxious.

"All right, though I'm afraid you came a long ways for nothing. I am a doomed man. But maybe my story can help you save my son. He signed himself a 'sheepman on the run.' That's fitting. We are both sheepmen, and we, like the others, have long been on the run in this god-forsaken cattle country."

Pete backstepped to his pallet and sat down. He folded his hands in his lap and said, "You see, this valley used to be all grazed by sheepmen. But a lot of them were Mexicans and fellas who had little money or education. Most couldn't even read or write. And gradually, cattlemen began to come spilling over from the Wind River valley. They had money and they had power. They hired lawyers, took over the best parts of this range, and shoved the sheepmen out."

Pete sighed. "There were some of us who fought. In fact, about six of us. But we didn't have much of a chance. They brought a couple of gunmen in here, just like the ranchers brought Tom Horn into the Power River country. Sheepmen started dying, flocks were poisoned, some were shot in the night, and others lit on fire."

"You had a range war," Jessie said.

"That's right."

"How come no one ever heard of it?" Bill asked.

"Because we were stupid!" Pete said angrily. "We should have got the newspapermen up here to see what was going on. But we didn't. We were too damn proud and stubborn, and all it got us were a line of early graves. Me and my boy, Mike, and our last shepherd, Dennis O'Toole, we're the only ones left. And Mike and I are wanted for murder."

"Tell us about that part of it." Bill learned forward, a small notepad in his fist, sharpened pencil ready.

"Not much to tell," Pete admitted. "There was this one gunman. He was as evil as they come, and I know for a fact he killed at least two of our number. Anyway, his name was Elvin Pattison and he was on the Winchester ranch's payroll."

"The Winchester ranch?"

"That's right. Biggest cattle company in this valley by far. They got the best land, the best grass, and the most water to irrigate with. Owned by a man named Ace Bard. You'll see him in court tomorrow. He also owns the judge and the sheriff. He's the power of this valley. And he's the one that had Mike and me framed for murder."

"How?" Jessie asked.

"I don't know for sure," Pete said. "But I'd guess he had his own top gun—that Elvin Pattison fella—shot on my range. You see, Mike and I came across him here in Skull Creek about a month ago. He got the drop on a slow old fart like me, but he didn't see Mike behind him. Mike just cocked his rifle and told Elvin he was going to kill him sooner or later anyhow—so it might as well be sooner."

Pete's eyes crinkled with pleasure at the memory. "You should have seen Elvin! Almost crapped right in his pants. He dropped that ivory-handled sixgun he was always showin' off and took off a-runnin' like he was chased by the devil."

Pete's smile died. "I heard that Ace Bard was so mad when he learned about the story that he fired Elvin. But what I think is, after he fired the gunman, he had him murdered and his body dumped near our place."

"I see. So your son had threatened to kill him sooner or later and then he showed up dead on your doorstep," Bill said.

"That's right. And that's all the evidence that's needed to get a hanging verdict here in Skull Creek."

Jessie looked at Bill Lamar. "Well?" she asked her new attorney. "How can you defend this?"

Bill looked positively euphoric. "It's easy! Everything is circumstantial evidence. There's no proof that the Bodies murdered Pattison. The threat and the fact that his body was found near their homestead is not enough to get a jury to convict someone for murder."

"Yes, it is," Pete said tolerantly. "And to make sure, they got a witness that says they saw me and Mike kill Pattison."

73

Bill's mouth dropped open. "That changes everything," he said with a deep sigh.

"Sure does," Pete replied. "It puts the hangman's noose around our necks and springs the trapdoor under our feet."

"Who is this witness?" Ki asked.

"His name is Melvin Dunn. He's one of Ace Bard's cowboys. You'll hear him on the witness stand tomorrow."

"We need more time," Bill said tightly. "We have to have more time!"

"Then we'll try to get it," Jessie said, understanding that they had to find some proof that Pete and his son were innocent of the charges—some crack in the trap that had sealed this man and his son's fate.

"Where is Mike right now?"

"He's somewhere off hiding in the hills or the mountains. He watches our flocks from a distance and helps keep poor Dennis O'Toole and our sheep from being wiped out completely. You see, Ace and the other ranchers, they come every few nights and slaughter another thirty or forty ewes. A couple of my"—his eyes teared—"my sheepdogs too."

"We'll stop that," Ki vowed. "Beginning tonight."

"They won't come tonight," Pete said. "And why should they? In a day or two, I'll be buried and all they'll have to worry about is Mike."

"That's the first wrong thing I've heard you say," Jessie told him. "Now they'll have the three of us to worry about."

Pete got up and walked over to the cell bars. Placing one of his rough old hands on Jessie's, he told her, "Honey, this old man ain't worth dying for. Not at all, he ain't. But Dennis is, and so is my son and our flock and dogs."

74

"We'll do our best," Ki promised.

"Thank you," he whispered. "Just don't get yourself killed. I can face up to St. Peter at the pearly gates, but I sure would dread meeting old Alex Starbuck up there and having to explain how I got his only daughter hurt or in trouble."

Jessie knew it was a desperate attempt to lift their spirits, and she appreciated the effort it must have taken for a man behind bars and almost certain to be hung.

"Here they come," Ki said, looking out the dirty window to see the sheriff and what had to be the judge striding across the street with a growing pack of lynch-happy men dogging their heels.

Pete nodded sadly. "You are runnin' up against the whole damn town, Jessie girl. I think you and your friends oughta just ride on back to Texas."

"The hell with that!" she replied.

Jessie turned around and faced the door. She was damned if this two-bit town was going to beat her, Ki, and young Bill Lamar. They weren't afraid of losing and they had not begun to fight.

The door banged open and the sheriff cocked his shotgun and bellowed. "Hands up! You are all under arrest for assaulting a law officer and obstructing justice."

Jessie glanced at the two men beside her. They both stood tall and straight and neither obeyed the sheriff's outrageous order. Their courage fed her own.

It was time to make a stand.

Chapter 7

Jessie's chin lifted in defiance. "Sheriff," she told the man, "I am beginning to suspect that you are an idiot. Put that thing away!"

The lawman stared at her with disbelief. He put his cheek to the shotgun's stock and hissed, "I'm going to kill you first and—"

The judge was a tall, stoop-shouldered man who looked to be in frail health. But there was nothing wrong with him mentally. He snorted, "This is Miss Jessie Starbuck, you fool! Kill her and this town will be overrun with United States marshals investigating her death. Not only that, but I will have you tried and convicted of murder! You *are* an idiot! Put that damn thing back in the rifle rack where it belongs."

"But—"

"Leon!"

"Aw, all right, goddammit!" the sheriff cursed as he stomped over to the rifle rack and slammed the shotgun back into its slot with the rest of the lawman's arsenal. "But you can't just let them ride in here and start pushing us around, Hank!"

The judge looked disgusted. He twisted around and saw a crowd of citizens filling the sheriff's doorway. He yelled, "Leon, disperse that crowd and then leave us alone for a few minutes."

The sheriff nodded and spent his fury on the crowd. He began shoving and berating them and, when the door slammed behind him, Jessie heard the unmistakeable sound of flesh striking flesh.

"Now, Miss Starbuck," the judge said, moving over to sit in the sheriff's chair and light a thin cigar. "Exactly why are you here and what possible interest is Mr. Bodie or his son to you?"

"I believe they are innocent."

"The court will decide that tomorrow."

Bill Lamar interrupted. "Your Honor, if it pleases the court, I'd like to ask for a continuance. Say, two weeks. That would give me enough time to prepare a reasonable defense and—"

"Impossible." The judge did not even deign to glance in the attorney's direction.

Bill shot Jessie a stricken glance.

"Judge," she said, "I notice that there is a telegraph office in this town."

"So?"

"So you will either grant a continuance in the name of equal justice, or I will spend the night if necessary in that telegraph office—I guarantee you, by morning, before you can even bang your gavel to begin the trial, I *will* have a telegram from the territorial governor of Wyoming demanding that you grant our request."

"I don't believe you."

"Test me," Jessie said. "I'd be happy to brand you with a monumental embarrassment."

"We might even be able to get a new judge," Bill said.

The judge whirled on the young attorney. "On what legal basis?"

"On the basis that you are prejudiced against the defendant, as is the entire town."

"Who said that?"

"The sheriff," Bill answered. "He said you would sentence Mr. Bodie to hang tomorrow. I'd say that a statement like that—given even before the trial—shows prejudice. Wouldn't you?"

The judge flushed with anger. "You young... you pompous young fool!"

Jessie raised her hand. "Judge," she said, "has a jury been selected?"

"This was not to be a jury trial."

"It is now," Jessie said. "We want two weeks to select a jury, and, if no open-minded citizens of Skull Creek can be found, we will ask that the trial be moved to Lander, Riverton, or even Rock Springs."

"You are pushing me too hard, Miss Starbuck. Much too hard."

"Judge," she replied, "you haven't seen anything yet. Now, do we get our requested continuance until a jury is selected, or do I spend this evening at the telegraph office? If I do that, I promise that you will spend the next month trying to get yourself out of hot water with the governor and several key members of your territorial legislature."

He was beaten. Jessie could see that the frail but vindictive old man in his black frocked coat was beaten. He wanted to challenge her, he shook with fury to challenge her, and yet... yet he was afraid. Maybe justice had once meant something to him, but that was long ago. Expediency, complacency, and far too much uncontested power were usually the reasons why small-town judges and law-men eventually lost sight of true right and wrong. Jessie knew that the entire United States legislative and executive branches of the government existed and stayed forthright and true to the Constitution because of a system of checks and balances—checks and balances that constantly regulated all branches of the government to ensure that democracy and the rights of the individual were always paramount. But on the frontier, the gun and the rope—they were often the final arbitrators of who lived and who died.

"Judge? What's it to be? We are not about to allow you to hold a mockery of a trial and pronounce a hanging verdict tomorrow to the cheers of a lynch mob citizenry."

He closed his eyes for a minute. He squeezed the long, thin bridge of his nose and blew cigar smoke into the air. Then he said, "Elvin Pattison was murdered in this valley. He was well known."

"And hated," Ki said roughly. "He was a professional gunman hired by a man named Ace Bard."

The judge opened his eyes. "I wondered if the famous Ki was ever to speak without first asking permission from his woman master. So, I've just learned that you do on occasion."

Ki smiled coldly. "Yes. And you cannot goad me into saying or doing something stupid in anger."

The judge's smile slipped away. "I didn't really suppose I could. But it was necessary to try. I meant nothing personal. You understand that, don't you?"

"Of course."

"Good. I wish I could see one of those *shuriken* blades which you have used to kill so many of Miss Starbuck's enemies. Or that unusual and strangely shaped bow, and those arrows. And our doctor would be fascinated by a

79

demonstration of your immobilizing use of pressure points. I understand you can render a man unconscious just by a touch."

Ki shrugged. "You seem to know a great deal about my weapons and skills."

"Enough to know that, if our fool of a sheriff had killed Miss Starbuck, he *and* I would surely have died within seconds. Is that not correct?"

"It is," Ki answered.

"May I see one of your *shuriken* blades?"

Ki shook his head. There was a faint smile tugging up the corners of his lips. "Nothing personal. I hope you understand that."

"Of course." The judge came wearily to his feet. He coughed, and it made him bend over in pain.

"You should not smoke cigars," Jessie said.

When the judge was able to speak, he said, "I know. The doctor keeps telling me that. But I don't listen to him either. I'll be going now."

"You still have not given us your answer, sir."

"You may have a week to select a jury," he told them. "One week from today, we will begin the trial and it must be held here in Skull Creek—where the murder was committed."

"There will be no trial unless it is a fair one," Bill said. "The jury *must* be impartial."

"That's an impossibility in a small town, Counselor!" the judge snapped. "Put away your damn law books and stare into the naked eyes of reality. A man has been murdered. Say what you will about Elvin Pattison, he was still murdered. All the evidence points to the Bodies, both father and son."

"That's a lie!" Pete raged, shaking his cell bar. "You and the sheriff are nothing but lackeys for Ace Bard and the other big cattlemen in this valley. You're on their pay-roll!"

The judge's mouth crimped and then he smiled cruelly. In a voice that would have charmed a cobra, he chimed, "He's a stinking sheepman. We used to have a lot of his kind in this valley. I wonder what became of them all?"

Despite the lingering warmth of this day, Jessie felt a chill pass down her backbone as the judge turned and walked away, very erect. She had to respect this man's intellect, and his final comment only proved he had black ice instead of blood in his veins.

Jessie, Ki, and Bill Lamar left the sheriff's office and found rooms. It was near the end of the day and Jessie was tired from the long, hard journey, and yet she felt keyed up and restless as she paced the floor.

"They are going to react swiftly," she predicted. "I have an idea that they will attempt to do everything in their power to thwart us in our attempt to get Pete a fair trial."

Ki nodded. "I don't see how we can get a fair trial in this town. Look out there on the street."

Jessie moved to the window. She saw crowds of rough men, all drinking and obviously angered by the news that the trial would be delayed a week.

"Some of them had probably ridden in from around the territory just to see a hanging." There was no sympathy in Jessie when she added, "Too bad they are so disappointed."

"Where am I going to find an impartial jury in this town?" Bill asked with a shake of his head. "And even if there are people who were capable of weighing the evidence fairly, I doubt that they would be foolish enough to vote their conscience. To do so in Skull Creek would be dangerous."

Jessie nodded. She had been thinking the same thing. "I don't know. All we can do is try and find evidence so overwhelmingly in support of Pete and Mike's innocence that no one could possibly convict them. And I'm going to telegraph a few newspapers and offer to help pay their reporter's expenses to Skull Creek if they will cover this story."

Surprisingly, Bill did not seem too pleased by that idea. "Wouldn't that be considered biasing the news?"

"What frontier newspaper isn't biased?" Jessie asked. "What we have now is a town that is in a hanging frame of mind. And we have a sheepman on the run who could begin to kill out of vengeance if we don't get to him quick and stop him."

Ki nodded. "He'll have no way of knowing that the trial has been postponed. It's my guess that he will probably come here tomorrow and try and free his father."

"I agree," Jessie said. "But I don't think he'll wait for tomorrow. If you were trying to free your father from jail on the eve before what could be his last day on earth, when would you attempt a breakout?"

"I'd want to do it tonight."

"Exactly." Jessie watched the sun set on the western horizon, somewhere close to the magnificent Teton mountain range. "And that is why we have to be waiting to catch him."

"He'll be expecting a heavy guard."

"I know that," Jessie said. "But you and I will just have to take our chances."

"What about me?" Bill asked.

"Sorry." Jessie touched his arm. "I think you might do

well to hit the books and get to bed early. Starting tomorrow, you are going to have some long, long days."

"But . . . but I can't let you and Ki take all the risks!"

"We won't be," Ki said. "Haven't you ever heard cases where the defending attorney suddenly died of lead or even rat poison on the eve of a trial?"

Bill paled a little. "Yes," he said. "I have indeed. My uncle warned me of those kinds of dangers."

"Well then, I suggest you be careful what you eat," Jessie said. "If you should die of poisoning, I would have a hard time finding another attorney before next week's trial."

"Thanks!"

Jessie kissed his cheek. "Good night."

He left them to return to his own room.

"What do you think of him?" Jessie asked.

"I think he means well and he has heart," Ki said. "I like him. But . . ."

"But what?"

"It was clear that the judge held him in low esteem because of his youth and inexperience."

"He's a good man," Jessie said. "And only a few years younger than ourselves."

"He seems much younger."

A smile creased Jessie's mouth. "Perhaps that's because we've been through so much together. You and I have fought a lot of wars, Ki. Big and small. Bill Lamar will too, but he's just off to a slower start."

Ki turned away from the window. "How do you propose to catch Mike Bodie down there tonight?"

"I don't 'propose' to do anything," she told him sweetly. "Why should I worry, when I have a warrior who has spent years in learning the ancient Japanese art *nin-*

jutsu, the skill of the invisible assassin? I would suggest you put on your *ninja* costume and go find our sheepman before he gets himself in any more trouble."

"What then?"

"Bring him to me and we can plan how best to help him and his father." Jessie sat down and scribbled a short note on the back side of Michael Bodie's letter. "Show this to him if he does not believe you are who you say."

Ki took the note. "I must tell you that, when we crossed to this hotel, I heard talk about another range war."

"Who's left to oppose the cattlemen?"

"I don't know. But someone said that other sheepmen were mounting a force to ride in here. They say that this land once belonged to the sheepmen and is best suited for sheep."

"That part is true enough." Jessie frowned. "But this would be the first time that sheepmen actually banded together to attack cattlemen. We can't let that happen, Ki. It could be a slaughter, and even if they were successful, it would surely generate repercussions across the West. All along the frontier, cattlemen would point to this and say: We had better wipe them out before they join forces against us like they did in Skull Creek." Jessie shook her head worriedly. "No," she said, "if Michael Bodie wants to do the sheepmen of this country a favor, he will not lead them in an attack. It would be disastrous for their industry."

"You can only kick people around so much," Ki said. "Sheepmen have been murdered and hounded too many years."

"I know that. But this is not the way."

Ki bowed slightly. He did not say good night. He simply left the room and disappeared.

It was almost dark now. Jessie stood just to the side of

her second-story hotel-room window and watched lengthening shadows join on the street below. If she were correct, soon a hunted sheepman would be slipping into town with two horses and a desperate plan of escape. And right now, Ki would be slipping into his *ninja* costume with its form-fitting black suit and hood. Ki would be able to filter through the men in the streets below and never be observed. Jessie would not have believed how the samurai could move in the darkness, taking advantage of optical illusions and his natural surroundings.

She remembered him demonstrating this skill to her, Ed Wright, and several other cowboys around the campfire one night. He had requested that they guard two horses tethered nearby. And even though they had strained for hours to catch his approach in the darkness, he had amazed them by suddenly seeming to jump up from the earth to land astride one of the unwary horses.

Jessie shook her head. She still did not know how he had moved so stealthily that not even the sharp eyes and ears of the horses had detected his approach. It was a remarkable skill, this *ninjutsu*. It was one that was used in Japan by assassins. Only this time, Ki would be using it to save a man's life instead of destroying it.

Chapter 8

Ki slipped out of the window and gained the rooftop by using a small ledge that even a wild tomcat would not have attempted to negotiate. He slipped across the roof and then silently hurled himself from the second story of the hotel to the one-story rooftop of a hardware and dry goods store. He landed softly, his impact cushioned by the steely springs of muscle in his legs.

Ki stayed low and moved quickly as he bounded from one establishment to the other until he came to the roof of a gun shop beside the sheriff's office. He crouched low and edged over toward the rear alley until he could peer into its dim length.

The alley was litter-strewn, and it stank from the defecation of men and animals. Dark, shapeless mounds of rotting garbage lay piled up behind a cafe, and he heard alley cats scratching and fighting through the rubbish.

Below and off to one side, he could see the rear of the jail, and he observed that there was no back door where a forced entry could be made. If Michael Bodie intended on freeing his father, he would have to do it through the front doorway.

Ki moved to the front of the building's rooftop and looked down to see that light shone from the window of the nearby sheriff's office. The man was inside and would probably remain there until morning. Ki would have expected that there would be a heavy guard out in front of the office, but there was no one, not even the group of drunken and rowdy troublemakers he had seen earlier.

The samurai edged back from the street and frowned. Something was wrong. The sheriff's office looked too vulnerable. Given that Michael Bodie believed his father might be sentenced and actually hung tomorrow, there should have been a *lot* of men protecting the jail.

Ki nodded. They were expecting Michael and had laid a trap. That was it! It had to be! What better way for the sheriff, the judge, and all the rest to solve the Bodie question than by allowing Michael to free his father? When they rushed outside, hidden guns would open up and the two would be legally slaughtered by gunmen waiting in the shadows. Ki was almost certain that the plan had been in effect before their arrival in Skull Creek. No wonder the judge had caved in to Bill's request for a continuance so easily!

Ki knew right then that he must stop Mike Bodie from reaching the interior of the sheriff's office. The samurai slipped back to the alley side of the roof and sat perfectly still while his eyes swept the murky darkness below. There would be men waiting back here for the young sheepman. They would allow their victim to bring his horses in and pass by to enter the sheriff's office. Their guns would not even be needed to kill Mike unless he somehow managed to reach this back alley where his horses would be tied. Then he would be riddled by gunfire.

I must find the men stationed below, Ki thought. *Every*

single waiting gunman in this alley must be taken out before the sheepman arrives. But how many were there, and where were they hiding?

He began to study the darkness until he sensed rather than saw a human presence. There, down near that old sycamore tree to his left. Two men at least. Ah, and at the opposite end, a man kneeling beside a water barrel. Minutes later, he perceived another waiting gunman behind an outhouse.

Any more? Time was running out. He wished he could have remained for at least another hour and watched the alley to make sure that he had them all located, but that would be impossible. The sheepman could arrive at any time. The samurai arose, his movement almost like floating. It was time to go down there and test his skills once more.

The samurai hesitated for a moment to meditate on what was necessary. He remembered his teacher, a very old, very wise master of the martial arts, who had impressed upon him from the beginning that the art of *ninjutsu* did not depend on the special black clothing he wore, but rather on the *ninja's* ability to meld into whatever surroundings he had to work with.

You must learn to use every feature of the combat arena, the old man had said. Train your eyes to see even the smallest things, the shapes and colors into which you can blend. You will see colors in the darkness if you are truly *ninja*. Remember too that few if any of your enemies will have learned the lessons I shall teach you—to find the dark corner of a small room, the shadow of a table, or the passing of a cloud under the sun. You must learn how and when to move so that your motion conforms to the motion of the earth, the constant changing of all things. You must press yourself to a wall, a tree, a single vine, and feel yourself becoming a part of that thing. And always, you must be ready to strike as soundlessly as a viper, as surely as a single shaft of light occasionally penetrates the hearts of even the most desolated among men. You must *become* your surroundings to be *ninja!*

Ki remembered and he perfectly understood.

The samarai moved back to the narrow alley between the gun shop and the sheriff's office. He dropped down between the two buildings and landed softly, then flattened against the wall.

The old *ninja* master had taught him how to become his surroundings, but he had completely failed to instruct Ki how to do this swiftly. In all of his practices, Ki had never felt so pressed by the immediacy of time.

He glided along the walls until he came to the edge of the alley. Ki was certain that those waiting below for Michael Bodie would not be looking for a man on foot. Therefore, he moved diagonally across the alley to a dilapidated fence. Now, he slowed and used his training to flow along the fenceline with grace and surprising speed. He could have made the same transition in broad daylight and not been observed except by another *ninja* master. The fence brought him up behind the two men beside the tree and he came at them with his hands upraised.

The first man took a knife-hand blow to the base of his neck and sighed as if with contentment as he folded. Ki caught him and lowered his body soundlessly to the earth. He had no wish to kill these men, only to render them useless.

"Psst!" the second man whispered softly. "Ed, I sure wish we could smoke. It'd help blot out the stinking—"

Again, the knifelike edge of Ki's hand sliced down to

find the neck. The man dropped in the dirt and lay still. The samurai crouched and moved off to find more of those who waited for Michael Bodie.

The man hiding beside the water barrel had an excellent sixth sense for danger, and it caused his head to turn as the edge of Ki's hand came chopping down. A shout of alarm started up from his chest, but had reached only the back of his mouth when the samurai's blow sent him into an even deeper blackness than that which enshrouded the alley. As with the two men by the tree, Ki disarmed this one and then moved forward toward the last man, who was waiting beside the outhouse.

As he stalked the gunman, Ki heard the sound of horses moving toward them up the alley. The waiting man whispered urgently, "Here he comes!"

That told Ki there were *two* men—but where was the second? He heard paper scrape roughly across exposed flesh and he knew the answer. The second man was *using* the outhouse.

There was no more time for stealth. Ki pulled his hood over his face so that nothing of his flesh showed. He was totally black as he ran lightly forward, his costume a dark and deadly shadow that went straight for the waiting man. So soundlessly did he move, and so fast, that he was attacking before his victim could give a warning to his friend inside the outhouse.

Ki's right hand shot out like a piston, and his knuckles caught the man in the throat. He made a slight strangling sound, and then he dropped. Ki found a pressure point and his thumb did its work. The man stilled.

"Hey," the one in the outhouse hissed as he quickly reached for the trousers wadded up around his knees. "What'd you say?"

The door was broken, and when Ki suddenly appeared framed in its opening, he was a black shroud. The man's jaw dropped and he stared with terror as the samurai struck. The man was halfway to his feet, but when Ki hit him, he sat down with so much force that lumber broke under his bare buttocks. He crashed through the stool-hole and his body made a soft splashing sound in the pit below.

Ki wheeled about and dove into the darkest shadows as Michael Bodie came riding up slowly, leading a second horse for his father. The man had definitely heard the outhouse boards splinter. Ki dimly saw him yank his sixgun from his holster and throw himself from his animal to land not ten feet from the samurai. The horses were well trained, and though made nervous by Michael's sudden and strange behavior, they remained ground-tied.

Ki was suddenly caught in a dilemma. If he called out to Mike, he might well die in a burst of gunfire. Mike, he was sure, had been on the run long enough to know that a man like himself was now in the enemy's camp. He would be inclined to shoot first and ask questions later.

But Ki had to stop him before he reached the front door of the sheriff's office and went inside. Once inside, not even the samurai could get him out alive.

Ki decided it would be best to wait. He flattened against the rear of the gun shop and sought the darkest shadows. Only his eyes moved as he watched Mike Bodie.

Mike did not possess the patience of a samurai. He waited perfectly motionless for only a half-hour before he went for the horses. He tied them and then, gun in hand, he moved cautiously over to the jail and stood on his toes.

"Pa," he whispered very softly. "Can you hear me?"

Ki's hearing was so acute he heard the straw mattress

protest as the elder Bodie eased on his pallet. The man made a faint scratching sound.

Mike spoke into the barred window. "I understand, Pa. I know the sheriff must be in there with you and you can't talk. But don't you worry. In a few minutes, I'll have you the hell outa that cell. There will be no trial tomorrow."

The straw crunched again and Ki knew that the old man would be desperate to warn his son away, to tell him that the trial had been postponed a week and that his son's desperate letter to Jessica Starbuck had been acted upon.

Mike turned toward the narrow alley that ran between the gun shop and the sheriff's office and which would lead him to Skull Creek's main street where certain death awaited.

Ki gathered himself to leap at the man and deliver a highly regrettable but absolutely necessary blow.

Suddenly, one of the horses heard a sound in the darkness. Perhaps a man that Ki had rendered unconscious had suddenly twitched. Whatever it was, it caused Mike to pull his shotgun up and point it right at the samurai as he leaped forward.

Mike pulled the trigger. His gun blasted away the alley's silence and Ki felt a bullet strike one of the leather-covered iron balls of the *surushin* wrapped around his waist, to deviate from a certain path through his vital organs. The bullet, however, cut across the front of Ki's belly about a quarter of an inch under the flesh. The pain was excruciating and the force of the impact spun Ki partway around. As he fell, he managed to grab Mike by the shirtfront and yank him forward.

They landed and rolled in the dirt. Mike pulled the trigger again. This time, the bullet whanged meanly off the rock wall of the jail. Ki took a tremendous punch that almost broke his jaw. He grappled for the sixgun, managed to get his fingers on it, and the gun fired a third time.

He heard a shout from the streets. In desperation, Ki slashed with the edge of his fist.

Mike grunted and the gun came free from his hand.

The sheepman managed to club Ki once more, but then the samurai's thick thumb drove into the man's neck. He found a pressure point and Mike Bodie stiffened and passed out.

The sheepman was a six-footer, but he was winter-wolf lean. Ki rolled the unconscious man off of him. He grabbed him up and slung him over his shoulder. Gunfire exploded in the narrow alleyway between the buildings. Ki snatched up Mike's sixgun and emptied it at the oncoming gunflashes. He heard a cry of pain as men reversed themselves and charged back the way they had come.

Ki knew he had about one minute to get Mike Bodie out of the alley. He could hear old Pete shouting for his son, but Ki knew he did not dare respond. So he ignored Pete and threw the unconscious man across his own saddle. Using the long leather tie-strings, he lashed Mike in place and then swung onto the extra horse and sent it racing ahead into the darkness.

Gunfire filled the alley. Ki held onto the reins of Mike's horse and let both animals run almost to the end of the block. There would be immediate pursuit. Ki did not know the country, and Mike would not be able to show him a means of escape. All around the town were miles of open range. It was out of the question to attempt outrunning the men of Skull Creek, with Mike tied across his saddle.

They turned a corner in a residential part of town and Ki did the only thing he could do. He drove the horses in across a lawn and through a vegetable garden into someone's back yard. Once shielded from the street, he dismounted, untied Mike, and pulled him to the ground.

Ki could still hear gunfire. Dogs were barking all over town, and lights were starting to blink on in houses. Ki lay Mike under some bushes. He slapped both horses across the rump and sent them racing away in the night. Less than a minute later, a posse came flying down the little street and boiled out onto the range.

Ki knelt down beside the unconscious sheepman and considered his next move.

A distinctly female voice came to him out of the darkness to say, "Just wiggle a little and I'll blow you to kingdom come, mister!"

Ki froze.

"Which did you fellas do? Cheat somebody at cards or rob the saloon?"

"Neither," Ki said.

"Well, mister, you musta done something real bad to create the kind of a stir that's taking place. How much money did you steal?"

"I need your help," the samurai answered, watching as the silhouette of a young, shapely woman began to descend a pair of rickety old porch steps.

"And I need your money. Maybe we can make ourselves a trade right here and now. My help in exchange for your gold and greenbacks."

Ki nodded. "Why don't you let us come inside and we can negotiate a price without the town watching?"

The woman was holding a rifle, and she used it to gesture toward the door. "Is he shot?"

"No," Ki said. "But I am bleeding and need some bandages."

"If you're the one shot, what happened to him?"

"He'll wake up before morning." More riders thundered past the house. "Please, could we go inside and turn down that lamp in your parlor?"

The silhouette nodded. "All right, but you make one false move, I'll blow a hole in you and take your gold away."

"I understand," Ki said, picking up Mike and carrying him through the open doorway. The house contained almost no furniture, no rugs, nothing but bare, creaking floors and walls. It was a three-room shack.

"That's Mike Bodie!" the woman exclaimed.

Ki turned to see her clearly for the first time.

She was in her early twenties, black hair, thick eyebrows, nice figure. But there was a nasty scar running from her ear to the point of her chin. It disfigured an otherwise pretty face.

She was as surprised as he was. "What... You're a Chinaman!"

"No," he said, managing to keep his tone neutral. "I'm a samurai, and I'm trying to save this man's life. He was going to break his father out of jail. The sheriff and the judge had set up a trap. Men were waiting to ambush the Bodies and cut them down in the street."

The girl took a step back. "All right. I know who he is, now who are you?"

"I just told you. I'm trying to help the Bodies receive justice."

"Then you've gotten yourself into a mess for nothing," she told him. "And so have I. You don't have any winnings or booty from robbing someone in town, do you." It wasn't a question.

"No," Ki admitted. "I don't have any money at all. And I doubt that Mike has more than a dollar or two in his jeans. Does that mean you're going to shoot us, or turn us in?"

"Probably a reward."

"Might be. But you'd have to live with knowing you handed over innocent men—possibly to hang."

The girl scowled. She cussed softly and then lowered the rifle. "I can't bring myself to do that. You know who I am?"

"No."

"I'm Sheila Abraham. My husband was a sheepman. Until about a year ago, we had flock that numbered over two thousand. But the cattlemen shot my husband, cut my face, and rimrocked our entire flock. You probably don't know what 'rimrocked' even means."

"Yes I do," Ki said. "It means they ran them all over the edge of a cliff."

Sheila nodded angrily. "That's right. So here I am in the house that my man and I used whenever we visited town for supplies. It ain't very damn much of a place, is it?"

"It looks weatherproof," Ki said noncommittally. In truth, the house was a pretty mean place for a young widow like this to live.

"I'll help you and Mike," she said, putting her rifle away. "I'd help the devil himself if it would get back at Ace Bard and those others." The woman came forward. "Here," she said, "let me look at that bullet wound. What are you wearing this funny black costume for, anyway?"

"It's not funny," Ki told her. "It is the costume of a *ninja,* a warrior-assassin from Japan."

"Well, this ain't Japan, mister. This is Wyoming territory and they look like a pair of tight pajamas. I can't help you if you won't at least strip down to the waist."

Ki stripped down. He looked at the nasty bullet wound

96

with more disgust than shock. Also, the leather covering of one of the *surushin* balls was ripped.

"Who shot you?"

"He did," Ki said, gesturing toward the unconscious sheepman.

"I'm surprised you didn't kill him for that."

"I told you, I mean to help save their lives. Miss Jessica Starbuck has gotten a delay of trail, and we have a lawyer to represent him."

"Who is Jessica Starbuck?"

"The woman I work for."

"You work for a *woman!*"

"Anything wrong with that?" Ki demanded.

Sheila shook her head and smiled as she went to get a basin of water and some bandaging. "Nope. I sort of like the idea of a man working for a woman. It's just kind of rare out here in the West."

Ki moved over and turned down the lamp very low. He peered through the window and saw riders charging up and down the street. He could hear them shouting and he knew that Mike's riderless horses would not have run very far in the night. They'd soon be caught, and then the search for them would return to Skull Creek. And the entire town could be searched in just a few hours.

I wonder if this woman will hide us? he asked himself. *I wonder if I dare to risk her life?*

She returned with water and bandages. Shaking her head, she began to wash away the blood. When she had cleaned and dried the wound, she tore the bandages into strips and wound them around his waist.

"I'm not much good at this sort of thing, even though the last couple of years I've had more than a lifetime's share of practice."

"I thought you did a fine job," Ki said. "You have nice, gentle hands."

"And you have a nice..." She blushed and could not continue.

"Nice what?"

She looked him boldly in the eye. "You have broad shoulders and narrow hips. I guess what I was thinking is that you are a nice figure of manhood."

It was Ki's turn to blush a little. And right then and there, he decided he wanted to get to know this young woman a little better. And that he would ask her to help them.

Chapter 9

"We need your help," Ki said. "They'll be coming back, and in the morning they'll search every house and business in town."

She studied him carefully. "Why should I help a stranger?"

"Because you hate my enemies for killing your husband and destroying your life," Ki said simply. Then he added, "And revenge is a very powerful emotion."

"So is fear," she replied. "And I *am* afraid of them. I know what they are capable of doing."

Ki said nothing. There was personal risk. Great risk. And he would not talk this woman into doing something that she would regret. If something went wrong, he would give his life to save hers. But she had to *want* to help them.

"I still need money—to get out of here and start over again."

"Miss Starbuck will help you with money."

"I never heard of her."

"Others have. Ask them about her."

"I will." Sheila walked over to stand near the unconscious sheepman. "I always liked this man. There was even a time after my husband died when . . ."

"When what?"

"When I thought he found me attractive. But he's always been secretly in love with Miss Carrie Connors. I told him he was a fool, but he knows that."

"Who is Miss Connors and why does loving her make him a fool?"

"You don't know anything about this valley, do you?"

"I learn fast."

"Tom Connors is the second most powerful cattleman in this valley. He and Ace pretty much decide how things go in Skull Creek."

"I see."

"Maybe you do, maybe not," Sheila said. "Tom Connors is tough, but he's no killer. Not like Ace. He still hates sheepmen, though. But Carrie, now she is a lady cut from a whole different bolt of cloth. She . . ."

"She what?"

Sheila frowned. "Even though her father is a cattleman, she almost seems to be sympathetic to the sheepmen. I've heard it said she has threatened to leave her father if he ever has a hand in any killing. She'd do it too. I think she and Mike Bodie know each other pretty well."

Ki wondered what "pretty well" meant. He also wondered if this Carrie Connor would help them if it became necessary. Ki filed the information and his questions away for future reference.

"Miss Starbuck is waiting to see this man," Ki said, as he pulled his *ninja* costume down over his bandages. "Since Mike is unconscious, may I bring her here?"

Sheila expelled a deep breath. "If she has a thousand dollars to make it worth my time, then yes."

"And if she doesn't?"

A look of vexation crossed the woman's face. "You don't cut a woman much slack, do you, Ki?"

"I have to know where we stand."

"Tell her to come with or without the money," Sheila said after a long pause. "But if they catch us here in the morning, we better be ready to fight to the end. The sheriff, Ace, or Ace's top gun, Dade Cocker, would all be quite happy to burn us to the ground. And this shack will go up like a stack of kindling wood."

Ki agreed with that assessment. "We'll have to be gone before daylight," he said, moving toward the back door.

When Ki returned, Jessie heaved a sigh of relief. She listened carefully and asked no questions until the samurai was finished.

"Can you trust this woman?"

"Yes," Ki said.

Jessie nodded. She trusted Ki's judgment, and so that question was settled. She pulled the curtains to her darkened room aside, and saw horsemen in the street. "Somehow, we have to hide Mike until things settle down a little, and then get him out of Skull Creek. Let's go see if he's awake by now."

They used the back stairs. Wearing dark clothing, Jessie followed Ki as he swiftly led the way across town. They arrived at the Abraham place without any problems.

Sheila was waiting, and even in the dim light, Jessie was deeply saddened to see how disfiguring a scar the widow carried on her cheek.

When she turned the unblemished side of her face to anyone looking at her, which she seemed to try to do, it was easy to see that the young woman was a beauty. Jessie knew of another similarly scarred young woman who had traveled East to visit a special kind of surgeon in Boston. That doctor had excised the thick, ugly scar tissue, and his surgery had resulted in an entirely new and very much happier woman. Under different circumstances, Jessie would have immediately suggested this to Sheila. But this was not the time or place.

"Ki said you were doing this for the money," Jessie said. "Here you are, one thousand dollars."

"The hell with it!" Sheila snapped. "I couldn't live with myself if I took it for helping poor Mike. Keep your money, Miss Starbuck."

"Are you sure? I can afford to pay you."

"I'm certain you can," Sheila said with an edge to her voice. "But that doesn't have anything to do with how I'd feel about taking it, does it?"

"I think he's finally coming awake," Ki said, hearing Mike groan. The samurai knelt by the man's side. He had to make sure that Mike did not open his eyes and shout before he had time to fully understand his circumstances. "Mrs. Abraham, I think you had better be the first one he sees when he awakens."

She hurried forward, knelt beside the sheepman, and cradled his head in her lap. "Mike," she whispered. "wake up. It's Sheila Abraham. You're in my house and it's safe."

Mike's eyes opened, but they were glazed for a moment. Sheila gently slapped his cheeks until he was fully awake.

"Sheila?"

"Yes."

"What am . . ." He saw Ki and his hand fumbled for his gun. Finding his holster empty, he tried to punch the samurai, but there was no steam to his blow.

102

Ki caught his fist. "Mike. I am Ki and this is Miss Jessica Starbuck. You wrote to her down in Texas. Remember? She has come to help you."

Jessie leaned forward. "We are all going to help you," she said. "But right now, we're in kind of a tight fix."

He was a tall, square-jawed man with reddish hair and wild, shaggy eyebrows. He wore a mustache but no beard. The first thing you noticed about him was the directness of his gaze and the deep throatiness of his voice.

"You actually came," he said as if he could not believe it himself.

"Yes," Jessie said. "Both of us did. You are very fortunate that Ki chose this place to bail off those horses."

"Dumb luck," Ki said.

"Not as much as you might think," Sheila said. "Although most of the families in this town depend on the cattle trade for their livelihoods, there are a lot of shop owners and townspeople who think that the sheepmen were badly wronged. Nobody will say so out loud, but after my husband was murdered and our flocks destroyed, for weeks I found cakes and cookies on my porch steps. I've come to discover that there are some pretty decent people in Skull Creek. What this town needs is a change of leadership and a change of name."

Mike sat up. He could not seem to take his eyes off of Jessica. "I saw your picture recently in the newspaper and it wasn't the little freckle-faced Texas girl I remember teasing when we were children."

"You've changed a great deal yourself," she told him. "I'm sorry that it had come to this before we got to meet again."

He shrugged and his voice hardened. "Nothing ever changes. It's the same old story, the rich get richer and the

103

poor get poorer. Anyway, it has sure been that way in this part of Wyoming."

"Maybe we can change that a little," Jessie suggested.

He pushed himself to his feet. "I'd settle for getting my father out of jail before daylight."

Ki told him about the trial's one-week continuance.

"So what good is that going to do? It'll just postpone the inevitable. The verdict won't change."

"Maybe it will. Maybe we can find some evidence . . ."

Mike shook his head. "Miss Starbuck, even though I'd been roped and dragged half to death by some cowboys the week before I wrote you that letter, I still thought maybe you could help me and Pa win justice and our freedom. But it's too late for that now. The only thing these people will understand is force. And that's why I wrote to several sheepmen's organizations asking for their help. If they come—"

"If they come you'll have yourself a range war and a lot of dead but well-intentioned sheepmen!" Jessie interrupted hotly. "Wyoming is run by cattle interests just the same as Texas and every other Western territory or state. You cannot hope to beat the cattlemen, not by force."

"So what do you suggest? You sound just like one of them—which you are. You don't give a damn about sheep. You'd probably choke on a mutton chop, or starve before eating one."

"So I prefer beef! Is that some terrible crime?" she snapped.

"And you'll always be loyal to cattlemen!" he said hotly. "Where's my goddamn gun and hat! I'm getting out of here!"

"How?" Ki asked gently as he stepped into the tall sheepman's path. "Your horses are gone. There are men all

104

over the place searching for you, and there is at least a two-mile stretch of sagebrush in any direction you care to look. But if you want to commit suicide, that is up to you. It won't help your father much, though, will it?"

Even though angry, Mike had to pause and then shake his head, admitting his foolishness. "No, dammit! But what am I supposed to do now? I've got a flock of sheep out in the hills and an Irish kid I'd die for, and they are in danger. I'm not waiting around here. I'll find a horse and I'll find a way out of this accursed town."

Ki looked to Jessie for a signal. If she nodded her head, he would stop Mike Bodie the very same way he had already stopped him in the alley. But Jessie shook her head.

"Ki," she said, "go with him. Help guard his flock and that young shepherd of his. Mike?"

"Yes?" Now that he was assured of leaving, he looked much happier.

"Who is the witness that is supposed to have seen you and your father kill Elvin Pattison?"

"That's easy. His name is Melvin Dunn. He's a cowboy on Ace Bard's payroll."

Jessie swore inwardly. "Of course. I should have guessed something like that. So there is no hope there unless we can break the man's story down in court. We'll go out and ask to talk to him tomorrow."

"To the Winchester Cattle Company!" Mike almost laughed out loud. "Miss Starbuck!"

"Jessie."

"All right then, Jessie." Mike stuck his thumbs in his waistband and said, "Jessie, that would be completely worthless and outright dangerous. You'd be trespassing on Ace's range and he could almost do anything he wanted

105

and lie his way free. I'm asking you to stay here where it's safe, in Skull Creek."

"I agree," Ki said.

"I'm sorry. But if Bill Lamar and I go alone, I don't think there will be any trouble."

"You say that, not knowing a damn thing about Ace Bard," Mike retorted.

Jessie couldn't argue the point. Still, she was determined to go. A week might seem like a lot of time right now, but it would slip away fast. She and Bill had to start turning over rocks if they wanted to find scuttling insects that needed to be squashed.

Jessie came over to the samurai. "Can you get him out of Skull Creek alive?" she asked quietly.

Ki nodded. "If he listens and obeys."

"Obey!" Mike said much too loudly. "Hey, I know I asked for your help, but I'm plenty able to take care of myself."

"I noticed that tonight," Jessie said. "You rode right into a trap, and if it weren't for Ki, you *and* your poor father would be lying in the street face down and riddled with bullets."

"There'd be guns in our hands and a few of them dead too," Mike said quietly, "and to my mind, that's a sight better than meekly walking up to the gallows and stepping through a trap door."

"We'll be in touch," Jessie said as they started to leave.

"Ki?" Sheila said.

Ki turned to look at her. She had placed herself so that the scar on her cheek was away from him. Ki knew it had been a conscious act, and this saddened him.

"I'll be all right. We both will." He touched her hand

106

and felt her shiver. "Thanks for saving our lives and helping. I'll see you again."

"I hope so."

When they were gone, Jessie said, "Come to dinner with my attorney and me tomorrow evening, Miss Abraham."

"I couldn't do that."

"But why?"

"I . . . I just couldn't. No. I appreciate the offer, but no, thank you, Miss Starbuck. Maybe some other time."

Jessie thought she understood. The poor girl was ashamed of her face, and probably of the fact that she had nothing decent to wear except old dresses made out of floursacks like the one she was wearing now. Jessie knew she could take care of the second reservation, but she did not know what could be done for the scar except seeing that Boston surgeon.

"Good night," she said, slipping out a moment later and hurrying into the night. She would try not to be seen by anyone, but she was no *ninja*, and Ki was not here to lead her. And besides, so what if she was seen? She would just tell them that all the gunfire and excitement had awakened her and kept her from sleep until she had decided to get some fresh air.

After all, this *was* a free country.

Ki moved slowly and took advantage of every shadow as they crept along, ducking into bushes and behind fences whenever riders hurried past.

"You're better than an Indian at sneaking around in the dark," Mike said with grudging admiration.

"Wait until we get out of here alive before you give me

107

any compliments," Ki answered as they came to a stop behind the trunk of a tall cottonwood tree.

"What do you have in mind?" the sheepman asked.

"I was thinking of making it to the livery and getting a couple of horses."

"They'll be waiting there for sure."

"I agree. But what else can we do?"

"Why don't we just jump a couple of passing cowboys that gallop by this dark corner?"

The samurai had considered the same course of action. He knew he was fully capable of doing it without allowing a rider to sound the alarm, but he was not sure about Mike.

Mike guessed his reservations and spat into the callused palms of his hands. "If you can hold your end of it up, I can hold mine. But we can't both jump the near rider from behind this tree."

"That's true. But what else can we do?"

"Give me a boost up to that first big limb and I'll drop down on top of my man."

Ki started to protest. The lowest limb was a good fifteen feet above the street.

"Come on," Mike said urgently. "I hear horses coming this way!"

"Why don't you let me go up there?"

"Oh, no you don't! It was my idea in the first place, and I'm going, not you."

Ki shook his head but he cupped his hands. When Mike lifted his boot and placed it in Ki's hands, the samurai gave a heave and the sheepman popped up. Thanks to his long arms, he was able to grab the limb. For a moment, he just hung there.

"What's the matter?" Ki hissed, listening to the approaching riders.

"This damn limb has ants or bugs crawlin' all over it!"

"Either get up or get down!" the samurai whispered impatiently. "They're almost here!"

Mike pulled his length up into the leaves. Ki watched him miss a handhold, almost fall, but catch himself to dangle upside down a moment before righting himself and climbing out on the limb.

The samurai shook his head. He should have insisted on being the one to climb the tree.

"Get ready!" Mike hissed, still fighting to keep his balance and not come tumbling out of the canopy of leaves and branches.

Ki flattened behind the tree, then peered around to see *three* riders. Fortunately, they were jogging their weary horses instead of coming in at a gallop. But there was no way that . . .

"Pssst!"

Ki looked up and saw Mike give the old thumbs-up signal.

The samurai shook his head in protest, but he knew that Mike wasn't watching him. How did the fool expect them to knock three men off their horses?

Mike answered that question with his falling body. At the moment the trio passed under the tree, Mike came hurtling down with his pistol in one hand and a torn branch in the other. He made a wild swipe with his pistol at one rider's head, and Ki was amazed to hear the unmistakable *thunk* of steel hitting skull. Mike made a desperate grab at the second outside rider and managed to grab a hunk of his shirt. The sound of ripping cloth sent the man's horse leaping forward and they both crashed into the dirt to grapple and claw at each other.

It was rare for the samurai to lose his concentration, but

he almost did this time. He didn't know whether he wanted to laugh or cry. He did neither. Before the rider nearest him could unholster his sixgun, Ki tore him out of the saddle and rendered him unconscious with a swift and completely effective kick that landed behind the man's ear. Had the samurai chosen to deliver his blow a scant half-inch lower, the kick would have snapped the man's neck.

Ki grabbed the skittery horses and swung into the saddle. He looked down to see Mike sitting astride a cowboy, throttling the life out of him.

"Just hit him!" Ki ordered.

"Oh, all right!" Mike raised his right fist. With his left hand still clamped on the cowboy's throat, he brought his fist down. When it connected, the cowboy struggled no more. Ki remembered how hard Mike Bodie could punch. His jaw still ached from their earlier tussle in the alley behind the jail.

"Let's get out of here!" Ki said.

"Suits me right down to the ground," the sheepman said as he disarmed all three men and stuffed their pistols into his trouser pockets.

Mike jumped into the saddle and they turned the horses around and headed for the western hills.

In a few hours, daylight would appear on the horizon. But by then, they'd be many miles away.

★

Chapter 10

There were so many stars shining brightly over the sage-covered hills that Ki could see quite clearly. Broken-away hills behind them marked the eastern boundary of the valley while just ahead, a low ridge of mountains marked the western side. And much farther up ahead, the country rose in a steplike fashion right up into the timber-covered Owl Creek Mountains.

"This is a pretty land," the samurai said, as much to himself as to the man who rode beside him.

"You serious?"

Ki nodded. "Down in the dry part of Texas, where Jessie has Circle Star, it is like this. A little drier."

Mike shook his head. "Hard to imagine it being drier. The only thing this country is good for is raisin' rattlesnakes and sheep. How long have you been with Jessie?"

"Quite a while. Why do you ask?"

"Just wondering. You and her ever, you know, get together at night?"

"No," Ki said shortly. "We're more like brother and sister."

"Amazin'," the sheepman said with genuine astonishment. "She's so damned pretty that just looking at her is better than makin' love to some women."

Ki chuckled. "I'd advise you not to make the comparison."

"No chance."

"How far is your flock from here?"

"About ten miles. I have Dennis move them every day as far as he can and still be close enough to water. At least, when the sheep killers come, we can make them hunt the first half of the night."

"How often do they attack your flock?"

"Two, three times a week. I try to be there, but if it comes down to dying and leaving my pa to swing, or runnin' and getting him out of jail, I always chose runnin'."

"I see. And when you run, does the boy stay and fight?"

"Hell, no! I make sure I get him and the dogs out before I go." In the starlight, Mike's face looked as if it had been carved out of a marble headstone. "The night riders don't want to kill all my flock. They know that's what will pull me back and make me easier to find. What I'm sayin' is that they use my own damn sheep as bait!"

"Maybe you ought to sell the flock. Start over somewhere else."

Mike peered over at him and said, "Would you let 'em run you off your own land?"

"No," Ki said. "That would be a dishonor."

"And I get the feeling that 'a dishonor' is a mighty big thing to a samurai. That right?"

"Without honor, what meaning is there in life?" Ki asked.

The sheepman rode along quietly, digesting the statement. "You know something," he commented, breaking a long silence, "I sort of feel that way myself. I could easily

112

end all this bloody business just by taking my flock over to Cheyenne and putting them all in boxcars bound for the slaughterhouse in Chicago. But my father and I have been building the quality of our flock for years. They may look like common old sheep to the unpracticed eye, but under all that dirty wool, they're pretty exceptional critters. If I gave up and sold them, it'd be admitting failure, in addition to throwing away five years of fighting off wolves, coyotes, blizzards and drought."

Mike shook his head angrily. "No sir! I can't do that! It just isn't my style. Honor is important to me too. Let the cattlemen have the Wind River valley, but God himself made *this* valley for sheep!"

"And rattlesnakes," Ki said, reminding him of his own earlier assessment.

Mike laughed. "That's right! I'd forgot the snakes."

They rode on another two hours, and when they reached a scree of rocks at the base of a rugged hill, they dismounted and climbed to its summit. Mike put his two index fingers to his front teeth and unloosed a high, shrill whistle that echoed across the hills and died just at the moment a dog barked.

"Over there," Mike said, pointing northeast. "There's a low spot between those hills with a spring and a couple of acres of good grass. That's where they are."

They returned to their horses and were riding through the sleeping flock and into the camp within fifteen minutes. Ki heard a dog growl in the sage, and then the soft voice of the shepherd said with a brogue, "Easy Dublin, Galway! It's friends this time."

The dogs' growls died in their throats. Ki saw a pair of beautiful black-and-white dogs move out of the brush.

113

They were border collies, long-haired and sharp-nosed animals of high intelligence and great courage.

"Dennis," Mike said, stepping down from the saddle, "I'd like you to meet my friend, Ki."

Dennis came forward. Man-sized, he stood almost as tall as Ki, and already had much the broader build. But he was young, no more than fifteen years old, and the fuzz on his cheeks shone in the starlight. He stood erect as if at attention, and then he bowed formally and said in his brogue, "Pleased to make your acquaintance, sir."

Ki bowed in return and took the youth's callused hand, and they shook. The samurai looked over at Dennis' bedroll hidden at the edge of the meadow in the sagebrush. He saw a rifle, a bag of potatoes, and a single iron pot for cooking. Apaches camped better than this.

"Ki will be staying with us, Dennis."

"No gun, sir?"

Before Ki could answer, Mike said, "He has . . . other weapons."

The expression on the young Irishman's face made it easy to read his confusion and disappointment. But he said nothing except, "Shall I boil you up some spuds, sir?"

"When the sun comes up, cook enough for all of us," Mike said, looking at the two dogs. "By the way, where are Queenie and Kip?"

The young sheepherder looked off in the distance. "I'm sorry," he whispered. "You weren't here last night and they hit us pretty hard. Went for the dogs, they did. The bloody bastards! Got Kip and Queenie right off before I could call them on the run."

Mike nodded. He opened his mouth to speak and then discovered he couldn't. He just made a strangling sound in his throat and walked away without comment.

114

Watching the sheepman, then looking at the two remaining dogs, with their eager, intelligent faces that waited for a signal or a sign, Ki felt his own anger harden.

"If they come again," he said to the Irish boy, "you take care of yourself and these two dogs. Leave the flock to me."

"No offense, sir. But what can you do without a rifle or a gun?"

Ki didn't answer. He did not feel there was any need to explain. A samurai never talked about his abilities; he showed what he could do by his actions.

As Jessie knew and others would learn.

Jessie was awakened very early by a hammering on her door. She had expected it, though not quite so early. "Who is it?" she called from her bed.

"It's the sheriff. We had an attempted jailbreak last night and believe Mike Bodie is still trapped somewhere in town."

"Then arrest him if you must, but let me sleep."

"Open up in there," the sheriff bellowed. "Every room and house in town is to be searched."

"By whose order?" Bill Lamar said from the hallway.

"By the order of the judge. Now let me look in your room too, young fella!"

"I want to see a written order before you are allowed one step inside!" Bill shouted. "Fail to produce a written order, and I'll have the territorial judge notified about your—"

"Goddammit!" the sheriff roared. "All right! I'll get you a damned written order. But I'm posting a guard, and neither you or Miss Starbuck had better try to leave!"

Jessie heard the sheriff clomp heavily down the stairs.

"Jessie?"

"You're doing fine," she called out to him. "Now go back to bed for a while. Your lamp was burning when I returned early this morning."

Bill turned away and Jessie went back to sleep.

It seemed only minutes, but in reality was closer to an hour before the sheriff returned with his signed search warrant. Jessie was ready to start her day. After taking her time dressing while the sheriff fumed and cooled his heels, Jessie allowed the man inside.

"I sure ain't got all day waiting for the likes of you," the furious lawman said, pulling his gun and moving right to the window. He glanced down at a sentry he had posted to watch and made sure that Mike did not try to escape.

The sentry must have shook his head because the sheriff scowled and then checked under the bed. Nothing. The clothes closet was open and there just was not anywhere for a man to hide.

"He ain't in the lawyer's room," someone yelled from across the hallway.

"Damn!" the sheriff grunted. "Ain't here either." He halted at the doorway before leaving, then swiveled around. "You know where he went, don't you?"

"Why bother to ask?"

"Yeah," he spat, holstering his sixgun and stomping out before slamming the door in his wake.

"My, my," Jessie said with a smile. "Musn't get yourself all in a lather, Sheriff."

After a leisurely breakfast and instructions from the liveryman where they had boarded their horses, she and Bill rode out to meet Ace Bard, owner of the Winchester Cattle Company. Most of all, Jessie wanted to see the supposed "key witness" named Melvin Dunn and try to get him alone for a few minutes in order to determine if she might break down his story later in court. She doubted that Ace would pick a weak-willed man to frame Mike and Pete, but she had to find out for certain.

"So far," Bill reminded her glumly, "we haven't got a shred of evidence to help the Bodies."

"This is only our first day," Jessie said. "Relax. We have a whole week to get evidence."

"Not me. I have to find an honest jury in a dishonest town. Remember?"

Jessie told him what Sheila Abraham had said about there being some honest people who were sympathetic toward the Bodies and toward sheepmen in general.

"If they're so sympathetic," Bill argued, "why'd they just stand by and let the cattlemen drive all the sheepmen but two out of this valley?"

Jessie looked around at the barren hills, the four windmills struggling to deliver pathetic little streams of drinking water now that the creek was almost dry. "Maybe," she mused, "they figured letting them out of here was doing them an honest favor."

Bill shot her a quizzical glance that turned into a thin smile when he realized she was taking the surrounding countryside into consideration and having a little amusement.

"Here comes a rider from the direction of Bard's Winchester ranch," Jessie said. "Maybe we can learn something?"

"Why," Bill said a few moments later, "it's the judge!"

"Sure," Jessie said between clenched teeth. "The old crook would have to explain to his boss that the trial and hanging were delayed a week. That probably was a very unpleasant job."

Bill nodded. "He does appear a little out of sorts this morning."

The judge was clearly upset about meeting them. He tipped his hat and started to ride on past when Jessie called, "I hope that Mr. Bard wasn't too upset when you told him the news. Wouldn't want him to cut your salary or anything."

The judge exploded in anger. "Why the hell don't you, Ki, and this here fancy lawyer go on back to Texas and leave this part of the country alone! Don't mess around with what you have no business messing around with!"

"We are here to help friends," Jessie snapped. "And to destroy you and your corrupt court."

The judge shot them a hate-filled look and whipped his horse on toward town.

Bill Lamar shook his head. "My uncle never told me it'd be anything like this in the legal profession."

"At least," Jessie said comfortingly, "it has nowhere to go but upward."

"There's Ace Bard's fenceline," Bill said an hour later as they came to a triple strand of barbed wire and posted signs saying NO TRESPASSING! INTRUDERS MAY BE SHOT ON SIGHT!

"Doesn't sound very friendly, does he?" Jessie offered, watching as Bill dismounted and struggled with the gate. When he finally got it open, she rode through and waited for him to close it behind them and remount.

Ahead lay a wide swath of the valley. Most of it was covered with green grass and decently fleshed-out cattle. Jessie noted the shining water trickling through the huge pastures. It wasn't hard to see that Ace Bard had enough to irrigate thousands of acres. His and a precious few other ranches were the only ones that looked suited to cattle as far as the eye could see.

"That must be the headquarters out that way," she said, pointing to a distant stand of trees and some buildings.

"You sure we shouldn't just wait for him to come to town?" Bill asked.

"I'm sure. Besides, we need to meet the prosecution's star witness and try to confuse his story. Remember?"

"Yeah. All right then, let's get this over with."

"It might not be so bad," Jessie suggested as they touched spurs and sent their horses galloping straight across the green pastures. "He might even invite us to stay for dinner."

But they had not gone a quarter of the distance when a body of six horsemen came racing out of the ranchyard to confront them.

"Maybe this is where the 'shot on sight' part of his fence sign comes in," Bill said. "I sure wish you'd let me bring a gun."

But Jessie knew what she was doing. If anything, they would be out to rid Skull Creek of Bill Lamar even before her and Ki. Without an opposing attorney, the case against Pete and Mike Bodie was open-and-shut.

"Just let me do the talking and don't let them rattle you into an argument or a fight."

"I won't be insulted, or let them insult you, Jessie."

"Just do as I ask. Please!" she said as the riders leaned back in their stirrups and reined their horses to a sliding stop.

"What the hell do you think you're doing!" the leader yelled at Jessie. "This is posted private rangeland."

"Are you Mr. Bard?"

"My name is Dade Cocker. Who the hell are you two?"

He was average-sized, but very handsome, with a square jaw and black, curly hair. He had dark eyes and good teeth and Jessie knew at once from his shiny boots and the fancy guantlets he wore around his wrists that he was a dandy and a gunfighter. No everyday working cowboy dressed like that.

"I'm Jessica Starbuck of Texas and this is my friend and attorney, Mr. Bill Lamar. We'd like to meet and speak to a Mr. Melvin Dunn. Which one of you might that be?"

Melvin nodded. "I be him."

Jessie turned to look at the oldest man of the lot. He was weatherbeaten and bent in his saddle, though she had the feeling he was still in his mid-thirties. He looked every inch a cowboy, in contrast to some of the riders before her, who had more the appearance of gunmen.

"Mr. Dunn," Bill said, "you say you actually saw the Bodies kill Elvin Pattison. I'd like to hear that story first-hand."

"Are you crazy?" Cocker shouted. "I ain't going to let you ask him a bunch of damned questions. Mel, shag on back to the ranch and ask Ace what the hell he wants me to do, shoot 'em out of their saddles or rag them the hell off his ranch."

Mel nodded and spurred back toward headquarters.

The riders relaxed in their saddles, probably noticing that Bill was unarmed, and not concerned about the gun resting on Jessie's shapely hip.

Dade eyed Jessie boldly. "You're a pretty woman," he said at last. "You gonna be stickin' around for awhile so we can get acquainted?"

"Only as long as it takes to free Mr. Bodie and clear him of all charges. Oh, yes, and to avert a range war."

"Tall bunch of intentions, ma'am. Damn near impossible to pull off, I suspect."

"I'm good at pulling off what other people think are impossibilities, Mr. Cocker. And I don't believe you and I are going to get any better acquainted than we are right now."

Several of the gunmen snickered with mirth. Jessie guessed it wasn't often that a man as handsome and flashy as Dade was snubbed by a woman.

Dade blushed with anger and turned his stare towards Bill Lamar.

"You still look wet behind the ears, Counselor. In Skull Creek, things can get a little rough for boys. I'd suggest you gather up your toys and get on back to whatever play-crib you climbed out of."

Ripples of laughter drifted between them, and Bill colored deeply. He desperately wanted to reply, but Jessie shook her head. Dade was just trying to provoke a fight. And if it couldn't be with guns, he probably figured he could intimidate or even beat the hell out of the young attorney and chase him from the valley.

The air grew warmer as they waited. An hour passed and Jessie knew that the delay was caused on purpose by the rancher. When he finally did appear, it was in a surrey, of all things—one pulled by a pair of the prettiest matched sorrels that Jessie had ever seen. Had the man not been their enemy, Jessie would have inquired about buying them.

Ace Bard was older than she had expected—at least sixty. His hair was silver but his face was very white and unlined. He wore a white Stetson, and over the hat the surrey afforded additional protection from the sun and heat. He was of average build, but his eyes looked like drops of pig-iron, totally hard and almost unblinking. He wore a suit and a string tie with a bolo that was carved in the shape of a longhorn steer's head. His hands were covered by white silk gloves.

"So you are Miss Jessica Starbuck," he said after studying her for several moments. "Why don't you turn your horses around before there is trouble?"

"We'd like to talk to Melvin Dunn."

"Mr. Dunn is on my payroll and I don't pay him to stand around talking to strangers."

"You've heard about the trial being delayed for a week, that's obvious," she said, glancing back in the direction the judge had taken to town. "It must be comforting to have the judge in your back pocket."

Ace paled a shade or two but managed to maintain his control. He chose to ignore the reference and said, "Your delay changes little. The outcome will remain the same. The Bodies will hang."

"I don't believe so," Bill said quietly.

Ace smiled. It was an unnerving sight. "You had best go away before you find yourself involved in a career-ending —even life-ending—act of great misfortune."

"Is that a threat?"

"No," the owner of the Winchester Cattle Company said lightly. "It is a *promise*."

Jessie had seen enough. They were going to get nothing from Melvin Dunn or this man. Not today, at least. And before things really degenerated into ugliness, she wanted out.

"We're leaving."

Dade Cocker looked at the rancher as his riders started

122

to goad their horses into a circle that would surround Jessie and Bill. "Boss?"

"Let them go," Ace said. "I have no fear of them. This is *our* domain. Let them live to see the Bodies hang."

So Jessie and Bill wheeled their horses around and galloped back toward Skull Creek without gaining anything of value. Jessie shook her head. What could they do that would help the Bodies in a place like Skull Creek during the coming days before the trial?

"We have to find other witnesses or somehow dispute that man's testimony," she said harshly. "We have to prove that Mike or his father could not have killed Elvin Pattison!"

"Agreed," Bill said. "But how?"

"I don't know. Part of the answer is that one has to lie waiting for us in Skull Creek itself. That Miss Abraham, she liked Ki but disliked me. We need her help. Only Ki can get her to talk. I think he realized that and will come in to see her very soon."

"She'd be murdered if she tried to come forward," Bill said.

"Not if she stays with the samurai," Jessie replied. "Her husband was a sheepman they murdered. Ki might be her only chance anyway."

★

Chapter 11

Sheila Abraham had awakened to the sound of men's voices in her backyard, early the same morning that Jessie and Bill Lamar had ridden out of town. Lying there alone in her bed, she had been dreaming of her husband, how he had held her in the night, caressed her body and kissed her with a growing passion that consumed her inner fires. He had been a fine man, a generous and loving shepherd who had only wanted to provide well for his wife and the children he had hoped to father.

Sheila had loved him deeply. Sometimes, in the night, she called his name and reached for him. But he was gone. She knew that he was gone during the long, lonely days. She could see his picture on the shelf where it rested. When awake, she could reason that it was only a picture. But at night, in her waking dreams, she did not reason and her yearnings tricked her into feeling his breath on her neck, his hands on her hungry young body. In those feverish dreams, he did not care that her face was now scarred, because he had always loved her.

"Hey, Sheriff!" a man shouted. "Come in here and take a look at this! Has to be their tracks. By God, they musta rode right through the vegetable garden and then straight across the lawn. Shod horses tore hell out of things!"

Sheila stiffened. The vision of her husband evaporated, replaced by a smothering cloud of icy fear that sent shivers down her spine. Now, the events of the previous night all came rushing back to her. The samurai and Mike Bodie had been running from the town and they had ridden their horses across her garden and her lawn. The tracks would be very evident.

Sheila felt her heart begin to hammer. She jumped out of bed, grabbed her old dress, and pulled it on quickly. The men outside would be beating at her door in just a few minutes. They would be demanding answers to questions she could not avoid. *What can I tell them?* she wondered frantically. *What can I say that might even sound remotely true?*

She fumbled with the buttons of her dress, and when she finally had them taken care of, she hurried to a small old dressing-room table and found a comb that was missing half its teeth. She fought at the night-tangles of her hair and then picked up a cracked hand-mirror and studied herself. All she saw were two frightened-looking eyes and the scar. She threw the mirror back into its little paper box and clenched her hands together. She squeezed them so tightly her knuckles went white, and she made her fear bank itself like the coals in a fire.

I must not allow them to fluster me or make me angry. If they know I helped the samurai and Mike Bodie, they will kill me, or at the very least . . .

The loud pounding on her door broke her thoughts and her resolution. She moved forward feeling as though her knees were sticks breaking. Absently, she wiped away the sweat from her palms on her dress.

"Who is it?"

"Sheriff Leon T. Pettit! Open up! I got a search warrant in my hand."

Sheila opened the door and saw five men standing tensely on her porch steps. "What do you want?"

He didn't answer, but drew his gun and knocked her aside as he charged into the house with his men right behind. He stormed into each room. When he was convinced that she harbored no fugitives, he came to stand before her with his hands on his hips.

"All right, Mrs. Abraham, where did they go?"

"I don't know what you're talking about. What is the meaning of this?"

"We believe that the samurai and Mike Bodie tried to stage a jailbreak last night. They were stopped and went into hiding. They later attacked and seriously injured three men and stole their horses. We think they might still be in town. We've had Skull Creek ringed all night."

Sheila lifted her chin. "Well, you can see they're not in my house!"

"But they were, weren't they, Mrs. Abraham?" he asked smoothly.

"No. Of course not!"

"You're lying."

She pretended hot indignation. "Sheriff Pettit, I demand that you and your deputies get off my property at once!"

"Where did they go?" he asked softly, stepping forward and placing his hand on her shoulder.

"Let go of me!"

The sheriff's fingers tightened. He moved close and whispered, "Mrs. Abraham, you're a young, ripe woman. Do you want me to leave these men here to find out whatever secrets you're keeping?"

She shivered under his grip. She did not trust her own voice. "No."

"Then where did they go?"

"They . . . they weren't here!"

"Sheriff," a man called as he rushed up. "I found this stuffed down in the closet. Bloody bandages."

The sheriff took them and dangled them before her eyes. "I suppose you're going to tell me you cut yourself last night?"

She said nothing.

"If that's your story, why don't you show me the injury and I'll help you to the doctor's office?"

"Just leave me alone," she said in a voice so stretched that she sounded addled.

"Where did they go?" he asked again, shoving the bandages to her bosom and pressing them and her back to the wall.

"I don't know!"

Sheriff Pettit smiled and stepped back. He watched the bandages tumble off her bosom and fall to her feet. "Mrs. Pettit. Sheila. I think we had better have a heart-to-heart talk later on. Maybe tonight, if I can wrap this thing up. Would you like that, or would you rather I arrested your sweet ass and threw you in my jail with old Pete?"

"Arrest me for what?" she breathed.

"For aiding in a jailbreak. "That's a damn serious crime, Sheila. You could even go to prison for it. Is that what you want?"

"She shook her head back and forth against the bare wall.

"I didn't think so." He winked again and smiled lasciviously. "I think we ought to talk about it later tonight.

127

Maybe we can work something out. Just don't you try and leave Skull Creek. Hear me now?"

She nodded vigorously. *Oh God!* she thought. *He's coming back to rape me tonight. I will never be free of him or this awful town!*

The sheriff smiled and then walked out. Several of the others gave her knowing leers and followed him outside. The moment they were gone, she raced to the door and slammed it shut. She heard their laughter as she locked the door and stood alone in the bare room staring at the picture of her dead husband.

She had to get out of Skull Creek today! But how? Not knowing the answer to that question, but believing she would find some way, Sheila began to pack, using a cheap cloth handbag that would hold all her worldly belongings. She still had thirty-one dollars left in the bank, but of course, it would be impossible to withdraw it without someone informing the sheriff.

I came here with nothing, and so I leave, she thought dismally. *But at least I told them nothing!*

Later that day, she had her opportunity. A freight wagon rolled past her house and she dashed out and threw herself into the back of it and then crawled under the heavy canvas tarp. She nestled among rolls of barbed wire and boxes of staples. She smelled lard and pickles. There were also apples and a block of cheese that she could not resist trying. Two men were driving up front and she had no idea who they were or where they were going. As long as the wagon kept rolling, she was safe and could stay hidden.

But later that afternoon, she realized with slow horror that the freight wagon belonged to Ace Bard and was heading for the Winchester Cattle Company. She had been along this road enough times to know it would soon cross through a gate and onto Bard's fenced pasture land. For a moment she wept silently and with great bitterness. But then she dried her eyes and climbed out from under the tarp.

She dropped soundlessly to the road with her dress folds laden with cheese, apples, and pickles. The freighter and his companion could not see her because of the height of their wagon's load. Sheila stood in the hot sun and watched the wagon grow small. Then she struck out across the sagebrush toward the Bodie land.

Running had never solidly entered her mind. She had wanted to escape Skull Creek. That done, she wanted to find the samurai and Mike to warn them of the danger they faced. And to ask them to allow her to help them fight the cattlemen.

She—and they—would all probably wind up swinging from a rope for their feeble efforts—just like her husband and so many of his sheepmen friends. But she was dead tired of fear and of being pushed and jerked around by every two-bit lawman and cowboy who saw her as nothing but dirt to wallow in.

Sheila hoped that Mike and the samurai had an extra gun.

Ki had worried all morning about Sheila Abraham.

In his haste last night to get Mike Bodie out of Skull Creek, there had not been time to erase the hoofprints across Sheila's lawn and garden. Maybe the tracks would not be spotted. Even if they were, they proved nothing.

But still he worried.

By noon, the samurai knew that all his reasons for not being unduly concerned about the safety and welfare of

129

Sheila were like muddy water—they had to be swept away to see the truth.

"I'll return soon after darkness," he told Mike and the Irish boy.

Mike nodded. "I could tell you've been worrying about Mrs. Abraham. So have I. Want me to come along?"

"No. You're needed here."

"We'll be moving the flock about eight miles to the north. There's a good little stream coming out of the mountains where they'll have enough forage to last out the week."

Ki followed his gaze. "All right. I'll see you there."

"They'll be watching for you in town," Mike said, giving Ki his Stetson and coat so that from a distance he would look like any other cowboy. "You're their number-one suspect in last night's thrilling escapade."

"I know that," Ki said with a grin as he caught his horse and quickly saddled and bridled the animal. He removed the hobbles, mounted, and rode away.

He took a wide loop toward Skull Creek, making sure to hid his tracks in a dry streambed where the rocks would leave no trace of his passing. He hated to lose the time, but there was little choice. He dared not leave tracks that would lead anyone straight to the flock.

It was late afternoon when he stopped a mile outside of Skull Creek and hobbled his horse in a small arroyo. "I'll bring you some oats when I come back if there's time," he apologized to the weary horse, noting that there was absolutely nothing for the poor beast to eat.

Ki moved into town the way an Apache stalks his quarry—low to the ground, in short bursts of speed, and utilizing every available bit of natural cover. When he reached the residential part of town where Sheila Abraham lived, he straighted and moved ahead at a normal pace as if he walked that street every day.

When he came to her house, he opened the gate and walked right up to the front door. Off to one side of the house, he could see the ruined garden and big hunks of bare earth where their running horses had chewed up the sod. *Dammit,* he thought, *we should have figured out something better.*

He knocked softly and heard the floor creak. The door opened and he said, "Mrs. Abrah—"

He never finished saying her name because two men with guns trained on his chest grabbed him by the arms and hurled him inside.

"Look at what we have here!" one of them crowed in triumph as Ki looked around the room. "It's the Chinaman, come to pay a little visit to Mrs. Abraham!"

"Well, I'll be," the other man said with a wide grin. "Now don't tell us you come to pick up the lady's laundry. Or maybe she ain't the lady we thought she was."

They laughed heartily.

Ki was satisfied that Sheila Abraham was gone. He could see drawers still opened, and the picture of her late husband was missing from the shelf. If she'd been arrested, they'd not have allowed her to take such things. That meant she had fled. But where? That was the tough part.

"Chinaman!"

Ki turned his attention back to the pair of gunmen. "What?"

"We want to know where she is."

"Who?"

The man snarled. He stepped forward and threw a punch at Ki's face, never thinking the samurai would dare to strike back, because he was covered by his partner's sixgun.

But he was wrong. Ki timed his movements perfectly. He took a sidestep, grabbed the man's wrist as it sailed past his face, then chopped the man's arm and spun him around to use as a shield. Before the second man could react, Ki had his *tanto* knife out and its long, thin blade pressed to the gunman's neck.

"Drop your pistol," he ordered, "or I'll kill him."

"Damned if I'll put my life on the line to save his," the second gunman shouted. He raised his Colt and peered down its barrel in an obvious attempt to try and shoot Ki. The samurai had no other choice. He was better at throwing *shuriken* star blades than his knife, but this was not time to be choosy. So he hurled the *tanto* knife, and it twirled exactly two times before it buried itself in his enemy's chest. The man's dying instincts caused him to squeeze his trigger.

Ki felt the bullet slam into the man he held before him. The gunman in his arms seemed to deflate. Ki released the body. It collapsed at his feet.

The samurai frowned. He had not wanted to kill. When their bodies were found in this house, it would create a whirlstorm of activity. But they had given him no choice in the matter and now the die was cast. They would correctly assume he was responsible, and he would be shot on sight. He was now as much a fugitive and wanted man as Mike Bodie.

Nothing was going according to plan. Ki hurried out the back door before the sound of the lone gunshot brought men running. The samurai dodged through the streets and then dove into the sagebrush that encircled Skull Creek. He heard shouts and then three quick gunshots that he assumed were made to call the hunters to the Abraham house.

But by then, Ki had gotten back to his horse and was unhobbling the animal. "Sorry about no oats," he said, untying the hobbles and swinging into the saddle. He stayed in the low places and rode out fast, wondering if he would ever see Sheila Abraham again.

Ki waited until just after sundown before he returned. He found her waiting for him at the new sheep camp. Ki felt a deep sense of relief to see that she was unharmed.

"I was afraid you might not come back," she said in a rush of words as she threw herself into his arms. "They told me that you were worried about me too."

"I was," he said. "I was afraid of what they might do if they found those hoofprints running across your garden."

She trembled. "The sheriff and some of his men came. They knew that you and Mike had been in my house. Like a fool, I'd not buried your bloodied bandages." She stepped back. "How is your side?"

"I haven't had time to even think about it," he admitted.

"Well, I have. We had better go to the creek, where I can take a look at the wound and wash it before rebandaging it."

"It's all right," he argued without conviction.

She took his hand.

"Hey," Mike called. "We got some beans and potatoes boiling. They are about ready."

Ki and Sheila shook their heads and strolled out into the night. They found a grassy place beside the stream, and she peeled his shirt away and then slowly unwrapped the bandage she had applied the evening before. "I wish there were better light," she said, tearing a strip from her ragged dress and dipping it in the cool water.

When she applied the compress it felt wonderful, and the samurai threw his head back and looked up at the stars. "Beautiful night," he said. "The stars in the West seem brighter than they ever did in Japan."

She cleaned away the dried blood. "You're going to heal just fine. There will be a scar, but nothing serious."

"A man with scars is a man with character. One who has lived with some danger and proven himself."

"Is that a samurai's philosophy, or your own?"

"The two are the same." He heard her rip her dress again and, a moment later, felt her rebandaging his side. "You should have been a doctor."

"I was happy just being the wife of a sheepman."

Ki dropped his chin. When she finished tying his bandage he kissed her full on the lips. For an instant, she resisted, but when he started to pull his head away, her fingers came up and entwined themselves in his hair. Her mouth opened for him and their tongues probed.

"Ohhh," she breathed, "I'm not a woman who can resist a man like you. I don't even want to."

"Then don't try," he told her as they dropped to the carpet of grass beside the stream.

As they kissed he unbuttoned her dress and found that she was wearing nothing beneath it. "Do you always go so . . . free?" he asked playfully.

"No," she admitted. "I was asleep when they came to my house early this morning. I heard them outside by the garden. I was so afraid. I grabbed my dress and put it on. There was no time for underclothing."

"I'm glad," the samurai told her as his skillful fingers moved up to find the soft mound between her legs. He explored for a moment, feeling her body relaxing as she

134

opened her legs wide. He slipped his middle finger into her and she moaned softly.

"Oh, don't stop," she breathed.

"Don't worry," he promised. "We'll have our fill of each other before the night is over."

"Good!" she cried softly, as she placed her hand over his and pushed his finger in deeper. Her hips began to rock under his touch and he felt her becoming slick and wet.

Suddenly, she began to shudder violently, and then her heels were raking the grass and she was biting back a cry that threatened to burst from her throat.

Ki smiled with understanding and appreciation. When the woman's body relaxed and went soft, he said, "You were very hungry, weren't you?"

She rolled over to study him in the moonlight. "You've just gotten me started, Ki." And to prove it, she groped for his manhood in the darkness. When she found it, he peeled his trousers off and lay back with his fingers laced behind his head as she climbed over him, stroking him into a proud erection.

She wanted his vest and shirt off, and he removed it gladly so that she could admire his physique. "You are a beautiful man," she said in a husky voice as her lips moved down his chest and across his flat stomach.

"You're a beautiful woman, Sheila."

"No," she said, "I'm not even pretty anymore."

Ki reached down and pulled her up so that their noses were almost touching. He rolled on top of her and said, "Don't ever say that to me or any other man. If you think you're undesirable, then you will be. You have a lot to offer just the way you are. All of us have our scars; yours just happens to be where it shows more. And even at that, you *are* brave and beautiful. You'd make any man proud to call you his own."

Tears glistened in her eyes. "Even a samurai like yourself?"

"Especially a samurai like myself." Ki kissed her, and then she reached down and clasped his buttocks.

"Take me!" she whispered urgently, "I need you so badly!"

He did not argue, but rather plunged into her yearning womanhood. She cried out with happiness. Her head rocked back and forth as his body assaulted hers with deep, strong thrusts. Her hips made music with his own and, because the night was warm, their bodies made sucking sounds to match the gurgle of the stream.

The music grew louder and faster as their tempo increased. Ki's mouth found her breasts. His teeth nipped at them and his tongue laved them greedily. She threw her legs up and locked them behind his narrow waist.

"Oh! Oh!" she cried softly, biting back a scream of pleasure. "Fill me now, Ki! Now!"

They came together. It was thunder and lightning, dusk and dawn, and a great symphony playing right beside them. Lost in ecstasy, they drove at each other until Ki sent his seed spurting deep into her lush body, which gladly milked him dry.

They collapsed and the music faded until only the night sounds of the prairie and the happy gurgle of the stream filled their ears.

"I thought I died and went to heaven," she whispered, clutching him to her tightly. "I wish we could stay locked together like this for all eternity."

He smiled at the thought and found it to his liking. But

the samurai knew the night would not last. Nothing so good lasted for very long. Everything had to be won in a struggle. And, at least to his way of thinking, the pleasure would be meaningless without the struggle.

Chapter 12

Jessie woke up and dressed with a deep sense of foreboding, knowing that her young attorney was in a state of near-panic. A week had passed since their arrival in Skull Creek, and today Pete Bodie went on trial for murder. They had made no progress at all on finding a sympathetic jury, or even one that would be impartial. Like Sheila Abraham, Jessie believed there were probably honorable folks in Skull Creek who would rule Pete Bodie and his son innocent of the murder of Elvin Pattison by lack of real evidence. But a verdict of innocent would place their own lives in jeopardy, and no one believed strongly enough in justice to take that kind of risk.

At least Sheila, Ki, Mike Bodie, the Irish shepherd, and their flock of sheep were all right. She had seen Ki on two occasions and was relieved as well as surprised to learn that there had been no more night attacks.

"They must figure it better to wait until after Pete is hung and Mike convicted of murder," Ki explained. "Then they can wipe us all out and say they were only trying to apprehend a murderer."

Unfortunately, Jessie concluded as she locked her own

room and moved across the hallway, Ki was probably right. It did make far more sense to wait until after the guilty verdict was handed down.

"Are you ready?" she called, knocking on Bill Lamar's door.

"It's unlocked," he called to her. "Come on in."

She entered, and saw him sitting dressed in a suit and stiff collar that she had bought for this occasion. Five days ago, when he had tried it on, she thought the dark, handsome suit made him look much more impressive and even more mature. But now, as she studied him sitting cross-legged in the center of his bed with books and papers scattered all around him, his feet bare and his eyes shrunken and dark-circled from lack of sleep, he didn't look very impressive at all. What he looked was scared, and beaten before the trial was even begun.

Jessie gently closed the door behind her. Young Bill Lamar just needed a little encouragement. She knew that he had been working day and night to prepare some kind of defense, but nothing was coming together right for old Pete Bodie.

"Bill," Jessie said, moving over and sitting down beside him, "the judge and the jury will probably expect you to wear shoes and stockings."

He barely smiled at her small attempt with humor. When he spoke, his voice sounded drained and defeated. "Jessie, we have an antagonistic jury and judge. They have a witness that says he *saw* the actual murder by our clients. And I don't have the least idea how any single one of those facts can prevent our client from receiving the death sentence. I don't even think that my uncle could have figured a way out of this one."

Jessie knew that everything he said was true. She had

139

lain awake at night trying to decide what she could do to save Pete and his son. They were both on trial, even though Mike was still at large.

If Pete won, then the sheriff would have to call his so-called legal posse off the son. But if Pete lost, not only would the old man hang, but it would continue to be open season on Mike. And sooner or later, they were going to kill the sheepman.

"Bill," she said quietly, "I don't expect you to be a miracle worker. All you can do is your best. I'll not ask or expect anything more."

"But we'll lose!"

"I don't think so," she said. "Ki and I are not in the habit of leaving Circle Star to come a thousand miles to accept defeat. I don't know how I can say this, given the overwhelming odds we now face, but I firmly believe that Pete Bodie will not hang and that before we leave Wyoming, they will be judged innocent."

"Not by this judge and jury."

"Then by another," she said firmly. "All I can advise is that we lift our chins proudly along with Pete, and go in there and give it our best. And if that fails, then we try something else."

"Like what?" he asked. "If the law rules—"

Jessie placed her forefinger over his lips. "In time, you will better understand the old saying that 'there is more than one way to skin a cat.' I won't let that old sheepman be hanged, Bill. Not as long as I believe in his innocence."

"I'd bet my life he has been framed," Bill said. "But if you are talking about staging a jail—"

Jessie kissed him on the mouth. He was startled for a moment, but when he reached for her, she jumped off the bed and headed for the door. "I'll wait downstairs for you

140

to take me to breakfast. We haven't much time, Counselor. So comb your hair, put on your shoes, and straighten that tie. And remember, *how* you're perceived in the courtroom is more important than what you know from the study of law."

"Huh," he mused. "I hope you are right."

"I know I am," Jessie said, closing the door behind her.

"Hear ye, hear ye, this court is now in session!" the pudgy bailiff shouted to the packed room. "The Honorable Judge Henry B. Allen presiding. God bless the United States and this honorable court. Everyone please stand as the judge takes his bench!"

The crowd grudgingly pulled itself to its feet. After the judge had seated himself and the jury had straggled in to take their places, the bailiff shouted, "Y'all can sit down!"

Jessie sat in the front row of the spectator section, behind Bill Lamar and Pete Bodie. Ace Bard and his men had filled the section to the right. When Bard had entered, the townspeople had relinquished their precious seats. Jessie could almost feel his dead, black eyes boring into the back of her head.

The room was hot, and even though every window was wide open, the air was very still. Flies buzzed overhead, and she could already feel perspiration beading on her skin. The room itself was stark and held only the rows of benches, the jury box and the judge's chair and table. The judged banged his gavel and called, "I pronounce this court in the Fifth district of our great Wyoming Territory to be in session! Today, we will try Mr. Pete Bodie and his fugitive son for murder in the first degree of one Elvin Pattison, whom everyone in this town knew quite well and who was generally well liked."

Jessie took a deep breath as Bill sprang to his feet. "Objection, Your Honor! Stating that Mr. Pattison was well liked is inaccurate, prejudicial to the jury, and completely irrelevant to the case."

The judge growled, "Sit down, boy!"

The audience laughed out loud.

"Objection. I am a practicing attorney, the legal counsel for Mr. Bodie, and my name is William P. Lamar. *Mister* William P. Lamar. I respectfully demand that the court refer to me in that manner. *Your Honor*. Or, when this trial is over, I will file a petition with the Board of—"

The judge squirmed and banged his gavel. "All right, *Mister* Lamar. You have made your point. Let's get on with the trial and try to wrap what is obviously a cut-and-dried—"

"Objection, Your Honor! That statement is patently—"

Jessie found herself laughing as her attorney raked the judge over the coals again. *Give him hell and don't let him get away with a damned thing!* Jessie thought, proud of the young man she had chosen. They might lose this case, but they were going to go down fighting. And she would bet that within the next few minutes the judge and the jury would realize that this trial was going to be conducted properly, like a court of law should be, or Mr. William P. Lamar was going to drag it out for weeks.

"Prosecutor, please summon your witnesses!" the judge called.

The prosecuting attorney, a man named Jeters, called his witnesses one by one. Each man took the stand and his oath and then proceeded to relate how they had heard Mike threaten to kill Elvin Pattison.

"Any questions, Mr. Lamar?" the judge asked in an acid tone of voice.

"No, Your Honor."

"Good."

Next, Pete himself was called to the witness stand, and after he had been sworn to tell the truth, he was seated.

"Mr. Bodie," Jeters began. The prosecuting attorney was a nondescript man who had a habit of pulling on his long, hooked nose. He shoes squeaked and he looked to be sickly. "You have heard the previous witnesses state that they saw, with their own eyes, your son pull a gun on Elvin Pattison and tell him he was going to kill the man sooner or later. You were there. Is this true or not true?"

Pete swallowed noisily. "Sure," he admitted. "My boy said that, but only because—"

The judge banged his gavel. "Just answer the question, Mr. Bodie."

Pete flushed with anger. "Elvin was a goddamn killer and he had a gun on me when my boy got the drop on him."

"Silence!" the judge barked, whacking his gavel down hard. "Any further outbursts from you and I'll have the bailiff put a gag in your mouth!"

"Objection!" Bill Lamar shouted.

"Objection overruled!" the judge shouted back.

The audience and especially the jury burst into guffaws.

Bill paled. When he spoke, his voice was stretched as tight as piano wire. "Your Honor, it is clear to me that my client has no possibility of receiving justice in this court. I therefore request that this trial be reconvened in Rock Springs before an impartial judge and an impartial jury."

Jessie's small fists clenched. "Good for you!" she said, loud enough to be heard by everybody in the packed courtroom. "This *is* a farce."

"Silence!" the judge screamed as he banged his gavel

down. "Request for a new trial in Rock Springs is denied. The Territory of Wyoming doesn't have the time, the patience, or the funds to play your silly games, Mr. Lamar. Mr. Jeters, call your next witness for the prosecution."

"I call Mr. Melvin Dunn."

Dunn came sauntering up. He looked nervous and out of sorts. He took his oath, and the questioning went very fast.

"Did you, on the evening of March tenth, see the defendent and his son, Michael Bodie, kill Mr. Elvin Pattison?"

"I did."

"Would you describe what you saw?"

"Sure." Dunn cleared his throat and called for a spittoon. He cut a hunk of tobacco, shoved it into his cheek and began. "I was ridin' home from doing some fence checkin' when I came over a rise. I saw the Bodies, and then I heard poor Pattison choke, 'Please don't drill me!' Next thing I saw was both the Bodies opening fire on him. I saw the puffs of black-powder smoke from their pistols and saw their muzzle blast. I heard Pattison scream, saw him grab his riddled chest jest as he was blowed right outta his saddle."

The courtroom was very quiet now.

"What else did you see or hear?"

"I was mighty afraid they'd do the same to me, so I dropped off my horse and led it back down the rise a few yards. I creeped back and watched as they rifled Pattison's pockets. I think they took some of his money and stuff."

"I see." The prosecutor looked very happy. He walked over to the witness stand and pulled a knife out of his pocket. It had a white bone handle. "You ever see this knife before?"

"Why sure! That's old Pattison's knife. Where'd you find it?"

144

"On Mr. Pete Bodie when he was arrested."

"I found that knife on my own range!" Pete shouted. "I found it!"

A hum of excitement shot through the audience. Jessie swallowed. She had not known about the knife, and neither had Bill.

"What happened after they rifled the dead man's pockets?"

"Nothin' much," Dunn said. "The Bodies just climbed on their horses and galloped into the hills."

"And what did you do?"

"I rode back to the ranch headquarters and found Mr. Bard. I told him I saw the Bodies murder poor Elvin Pattison. He sent a wagon out for the body and we carted it to the mortician. He did a real nice job on poor Elvin. Layin' in that coffin with a new shirt on and a white collar, he sure looked a lot finer dead than he did when he was alive."

"Thank you," the attorney said. "That will be all. You may cross-examine the witness, Mr. Lamar."

Bill arose slowly. "You say that you actually *saw* them shoot Elvin Pattison?"

Dunn had stopped smiling. He was on his guard now. "That's what I said."

"How far away were you?"

Dunn shrugged. "I didn't pace it off. Maybe half a mile? Close enough to see the smoke from their muzzles and see their faces clear."

"I see. Are you aware that Mr. Bodie and his son had purchased the new *cartridge*-loading sixguns the week before, and had traded in their old black-powder pistols?"

Dunn's eyes widened. "I saw black-powder smoke!"

"Easy to prove one way or the other," Bill said. "We just exhume the body and have the bullets dug out of it.

145

They are either lead balls shot by black powder or they are lead slugs from a cartridge. I think that would prove you are telling the truth or lying—one way or the other—don't you?"

"Objection!" Jeters cried. "The witness actually saw the murder. Whether or not he is correct in stating he saw black-powder smoke is immaterial."

"Objection sustained," the judge said a little nervously.

The courtroom buzzed. Dunn shifted uncomfortably in his chair and Bill Lamar seethed. "Mr. Dunn," he said, "you testified under oath that you heard Mr. Pattison beg for his life just before he was murdered by the Bodies. Is that correct?"

Dunn shot a glance at Ace Bard, who sat off to one side of the courtroom, and whose white face was now filled with contempt.

"Is that correct?" Bill repeated.

"Yes."

"At about a half-mile, you heard Pattison choke, 'Don't drill me'?"

Now Dunn saw the trap. "Might not have been a half-mile. Mighta been a little closer."

Bill stabbed a finger at him. "You couldn't hear me speaking from across the street! Let alone a half-mile, a quarter-mile or even a lousy hundred yards!"

He whirled to face the jury. "Gentlemen, we have just heard this supposedly key witness perjure himself at least twice. Not only did he not *see* smoke but he did not *hear* anything. He did neither because this whole story is a pathetic and shoddy lie in a sorry attempt to hang two innocent sheepmen!"

"Objection, Your Honor! The defense is badgering my witness and confusing him."

The judge looked shaken. "Objection sustained. Strike the witness's cross-examination from the record."

"Your Honor!" Bill shouted, "how in the name of justice am I . . ."

The judge's gavel began to bang on the poker table, and he yelled, "You are out of order! You are in contempt of court. I fine you one hundred dollars. The next time, it'll be two hundred."

Jessie had seen enough. Her attorney had clearly proven that Melvin Dunn was a liar whose testimony was shot full of holes. This court was impossible.

She came to her feet and hurled a hundred-dollar bill at the fat bailiff. "This court is a mockery of justice," she cried, "a travesty we will not endure another minute."

"You are not in charge here," the judge roared, "I am! Jury, you have heard enough of this nonsense. Have you reached a verdict?"

"We have, Your Honor."

"Then what is it?"

"Guilty as charged for both father and son."

Bill Lamar shouted, "It hasn't been proven that this is the man whose bullet killed Elvin Pattison! It could even have been Michael's bullets! Your Honor, if you sentence this man to hang, the verdict will be challenged and I will demand that the body of Elvin Pattison be exhumed."

The judge glared at him. "Be sorta like having the gate closed after the cows run out, wouldn't it?"

"You'll be disbarred if Pete Bodie has been executed by your orders. We will use every recourse available to drive you from the bench forever!"

The judge frowned. "Perhaps I had better take this under consideration tonight. I believe in justice, and it might be that a twenty-year sentence is in order. Yes sir, I am capable of leniency."

"Leniency! Twenty years!" Jessie cried. "That would be a death sentence. At Mr. Bodie's age, you know he'd die before he got parole."

Now the judge looked happy again. "The court can't help it if he's old. The law says a sentence can't be decided on the basis of a man's natural lifespan. I can't give an old man less of a sentence than a young one for the same crime, now can I?"

Bill Lamar's shoulders sagged. Though this bought them time to appeal, it was also the kind of sentence they had both dreaded. If there was a death sentence, Jessie knew that she could telegraph the territorial governor and the newspapers. With all the attention and the unusual circumstances, the governor would probably declare a mistrial and do it tonight. But a twenty-year sentence was another thing entirely. And Bill was right—it was the equivalent of a slow death for the old shepherd.

The judge banged his gavel down hard. "This court will reconvene at ten o'clock in the morning for sentencing. The court is adjourned."

Bill and Jessie watched helplessly as Pete was led away in shackles. Ace Bard was smiling as he headed for the judge's chambers. Twenty years for the father also meant twenty years for the son. Either way, it would be the end of the Bodies and the last of the hated sheepmen.

Jessie twisted away feeling defeated. It was all slipping through their fingers. They were in need of a miracle.

Chapter 13

The courtroom was packed and very quiet the next morning. Jessie had spent all night at the telegraph office. Not only had she sent a four-page telegram to the territorial governor of Wyoming, but shorter telegrams to many of its legislators as well. Her father had once owned land in this county before he had consolidated his cattle empire down in Texas. Alex Starbuck had been on a first-name basis with some of the most powerful men in Wyoming, and Jessie knew that his name still carried weight in these parts.

For insurance, and because she was not the kind of woman to leave any stone unturned, Jessie had also contacted the *Denver Daily,* the *Laramie Herald,* and the *Cheyenne News*. She had offered to pay travel expenses for any newsman who could come at once to Skull Creek. Now, each of those three newspapers was dispatching its best reporter this very day.

So now, as Jessie watched the judge enter the courtroom and heard the bailiff ask them all to stand, she guessed that she'd done all that she could. And despite everything that had been done up to now, it seemed almost certain that the judge would sentence Pete and his son to a twenty-year prison sentence.

"This court will come to order," the judge called, banging his gavel down and staring at the defendent. "This court has put considerable thought to the sentence it shall impose. Mr. Peter Bodie, you and your fugitive son have been found guilty by the jury. You are both hotheaded and headstrong. I myself once warned you to leave Skull Creek and these environs. You should have taken that advice. Instead, you threatened to start a range war between the cattlemen and the sheepmen. In short, Mr. Bodie, you've been obstinate and a troublemaker."

Pete spat on the floor. "Me and my boy have as much right to this valley as you, Ace, Tom Connor, or any other man in this courtroom. I fought for what was mine."

The judge shook his head. "No, I believe that the jury and my own sense of things tells me that you Bodies were always the ones that were the source of the trouble."

"Objection!" Bill Lamar shouted. "This isn't a sentencing. This is a lecture so full of vindictive poison that it gags me. My client does not have to take a tongue-lashing from you or any—"

The judge's face twisted up, and he shouted, "Bailiff, arrest that young fool and have him bound over to the sheriff for sentencing next week on account of his disrupting this here court!"

"You can't do that!" Jessie shouted, coming to her feet. "That is the defense's attorney!"

"I can do it and I have done it!" the judge snorted. "And if you open your mouth once more, Miss Starbuck, I'll have you arrested as well!"

The bailiff came at Bill, and the young attorney punched him in the nose. The nose broke and blood

150

sheeted down the bailiff's face. The man covered his face with his hands and sat down as the sheriff and two other men jumped forward, grabbed Bill, and hauled him kicking and shouting out the door.

Jessie forced herself to stay rooted in one place. The judge was eyeballing her, daring her to interfere so that he could also have her arrested—arrested and thrown in jail where she would be no help at all to Pete and Michael Bodie. It took all the steel she had to keep her silence.

The judge was obviously disappointed in Jessie's lack of response. "All right, then," he said, lowering his voice as he banged his gavel down once more. "I hereby sentence both Peter Bodie and his son to twenty years in the territorial prison. This man is to be transported to the prison tomorrow and a one-thousand-dollar reward is to be placed on the head of his son as of this very day."

The judge almost smiled as he added, "The reward is for him to be taken dead or alive."

Jessie was stunned. Even the people of Skull Creek seemed shocked, and Jessie heard their mutterings.

"Dead or alive!" the judge yelled, slamming his gavel down once more.

"No! This is wrong!"

All heads turned to see Carrie Connors surge to her feet. She was pale, and her voice shook with outrage and helpless fury. "The Bodies are entirely innocent! They couldn't possibly have murdered Elvin Pattison on the night of March tenth because I was with them!"

"What?" the girl's father, Tom Connors, shouted. "You sit down and shut up!"

But the girl rushed up to the witness stand, where she whirled and faced the stunned courtroom. "I'm sorry, Father, but I can't let this go on any longer. I am in love with

Michael! I spent that night with him. And—I have to ask or I think I'll go crazy—where were you?"

Following her question, the audience erupted into shouts and arguments; it took the judge several minutes to restore order.

Now Tom Connors was on his feet. He was tall, broad-shouldered, and rugged in appearance. But right at the moment, what he looked like mostly was shocked and in pain. As debates raged all around him, he stood like a tree and seemed oblivious to everything but his daughter. Yet his first words had the same effect on the arguments as a bucket of water had on a campfire. The talk died out as quickly as it had started. "I was in Cheyenne that whole week, just like I told you."

Jessie came to her feet. With Bill in jail, she had to ask the questions. "Can you prove that?"

"Hell yes I can!" Tom Connors raged. "Your're damn right I can. That night I had dinner with Russ Watley and his family. He's the mayor of Cheyenne and the town's biggest banker."

For some reason, Jessie was relieved. She had not wanted any more men caught up in this treachery. From the look on Carrie Connors' face, it was obvious that the girl was satisfied as well. She looked ready to weep.

Connors, however, was anything but relieved, "Carrie," he said, "the thing that plain stumps and pains me is that I ordered you never to even think about that Michael Bodie."

"I don't care what you say anymore!" she cried.

"I'm twenty years old. I'm a woman—one that loves Michael. And I *was* with him that night. We slept together less than a hundred yards from his father. The camp was at Coyote Springs and, since Mr. Pattison's body was found

152

almost ten miles from there, Michael and his father *have* to be innocent!"

"Why didn't you say that right at the start?" Jessie asked the poor, distraught girl. "It would have made everything so easy."

She looked right at Jessie. "Because Michael made me swear never to tell, and because I was afraid that, if my father knew, he would kill them both."

The judge banged his gavel down hard. "This court cannot accept the testimony of a girl who has lied to her own father and is obviously not in a stable frame of mind. The verdict and my sentence stand!"

"No they won't," Jessie said, "and your days as a judge are now over."

The judge pointed a finger at her and shook it accusingly. "Damn you, Miss Starbuck! You should never have left Texas!"

Jessie whirled around to see Ace Bard, Dade Cocker, and the sheriff moving toward Tom Connors, who was bulling his way outside. Dade tried to grab Connors by the shirt, but the much larger man slung his hand away in fury.

"Father!" Carrie shouted in a voice that cut across the room, "please don't go hunting for Michael! It wasn't his fault! I love him!"

But Tom Connors wasn't listening. Knocking people aside in his fury, the Wyoming cattleman stormed outside and vanished.

Jessie turned to see the girl dissolve in tears.

It had taken a lot of courage to stand up before this courtroom and confess to sleeping with a sheepman, the avowed enemy of her father. But what had it gained? The judge's sentence stood. And now it seemed to Jessie that they had one more man to worry about. It certainly appeared, from the look on Tom Connors' rugged face, that he was going to do Ace Bard's work for him.

Ace Bard stood beside the hitchrail with his thumbs hooked into his tooled leather belt. Behind him stood his big ranch house with its fancy porch. The door was made of some kind of wood imported from Europe, inlaid with silver and mother-of-pearl. The design was a Winchester rifle with Ace's brand and initials carved into it.

The rancher was smiling. "It's working out just perfect, Dade. All you have to do is let Tom Connor kill Mike Bodie, and then you make sure that the Chinaman and the rest of them end up the same way. We can frame Tom and, before this is all over, we'll have his spread as well as the Bodie range."

"You'll own most all this valley, then," Dade said, trying hard to keep a note of jealousy out of his voice. "Seems to me you ought to give me a piece of the cake too."

Ace's expression did not change. "You see me through on this," he replied, "you'll share in our good fortune. I'll make it right by you."

"I'll want more than just cash," Dade said quickly. "And so will whoever else I pick to ride out and slaughter a woman, a boy, that Chinaman, and some dogs."

Ace reached inside his pocket and selected two good Havana cigars. He gave one to Dade, saying, "Don't get greedy on me. I can stand anything but greed."

Dade lit his cigar and decided he had better not push the cattleman. It was his experience that Ace Bard was tight-fisted but reasonable, unless crossed. Dade did not want to ride out worrying if he had made another enemy and if he was still working for the brand. He decided it would be smart to load on a bit of flattery. Ace had more pride than sagebrush. "Ace, I swear you're gonna be so big you'll own this whole valley after too long."

"That's the way I see it," Ace said, inhaling smoke as his foreman lit his cigar before touching a match to his own. "I figure to spill on over these hills into the Wind River valley and give them sonsabitches something to talk about."

"You never forgave 'em for running you out of that valley, did you?" Dade and everyone else who worked for the brand knew that Ace Bard lived and breathed in order to return to the Wind River and squash the very men who had driven him out.

"They made a mistake and it cost me my wife. We didn't want much, but they pushed us right over that ridge of hills into this valley. When my Sarah died, I knew hell. Then, little by little, I decided that the thing to do was to get even, and that being a big fish in a small pond wasn't so bad."

"I sure wish that damned Carrie hadn't spoken up like that," Dade grunted. "I sorta had my eye on her myself."

"You and every cowboy in this and the Wind River valley. She must be mighty sick to favor a sheepman over a cattleman." Ace shook his head. "I never seen a man so shocked as Tom Connor was this morning. If she'd have beat him with a blacksmith's hammer, it wouldn't have hurt him any more."

"If I had a daughter did that to me," Dade said, working up to a slow anger, "I'd shoot her dead and throw her body to the hogs."

Ace chuckled at that. "I almost believe you would."

"I hate sheep worse than flies and mosquitos."

"You better ride on out now. Take Charley and Gus for the job."

Dade frowned and said, "Quirt Taylor is faster with a gun." Quirt, he knew, was also more inclined to take orders without question.

"That's true enough," Ace agreed. "But Quirt is too young and eager. Besides, I have other plans for him."

"What other plans?"

"He'll be paying a visit to old Pete. A little surprise we've cooked up."

The "surprise" would be a bullet. Dade had expected to do the job himself. Shooting a defenseless old man was about as appealing as shooting a kid and Sheila Abraham. But he was going to be well paid for the work, and he had never backed out of the job because of squeamishness yet. "You don't miss a trick, do you?"

Ace shook his head. "I play to win and I cover all my bets. Besides," he added, "Charley and Gus are steadier, and better rifle shots."

Dade just nodded. "We'll be back tomorrow. Then you can head for the land office and file. Why don't you put about five thousand acres along the creek in my name?"

Ace exhaled cigar smoke and said, "My, my, but you are getting hungry, aren't you Dade." It wasn't a question; it was a fact.

"You damn sure don't have to worry that I'd ever buy woolies and run 'em next to your range."

"Bury the bodies and brush out your tracks comin' and goin'," Ace told him.

Dade nodded before he reined his horse around and dug in his spurs. Ace had ordered him to take Charley and Gus, but had not outlined how he wanted the job done. All he had said was that he wanted no witnesses.

Chapter 14

Ki had a feeling that trouble was coming his way. The feeling was not something that was easily definable, but he had learned never to ignore it.

Twice, their flock had been attacked in the night, but the raids were more like probes — hit-and-run, and obviously not staged with the intention of doing anything more than killing a few sheep, and harrassing Ki and the others into getting as little sleep as possible. Fortunately, the samurai was not a man who required much sleep.

Ki looked over toward the western horizon and a blood-red sun that would soon be going down. He had not heard from Jessie in almost a week. Instead of watching her, he was protecting a bunch of bleating sheep. Ki had decided he did not like sheep very much. They were stupid beyond belief. They would get lost or trapped in brush, and then simply stand and bleat until someone came to help them out of whatever predicament they had gotten themselves into. The poor sheepdogs were constantly at work, driving them from pasture to waterhole and back to pasture. The best that could be said about sheep was that they were not bright enough to be devious, or courageous enough to be adventuresome.

If he disliked the woolies themselves, he had developed a tremendous regard for the beautiful border collies that Mike and Dennis used to such great advantage. The dogs were tireless and, when they sensed danger, absolutely fearless. They would attack wolves, probably even a grizzly bear if one charged their flock. They were the most intelligent animals Ki had ever seen, and seemed to read their master's thoughts even before a hand signal or a sharp whistle was given. Watching Dublin and Galway work was a real pleasure.

Sheila finished up the dinner dishes and came to stand beside him. She slipped her arm around his waist. "You seem restless tonight."

"I am," he said. "I want you to sleep near that line of sage instead of out in the open. Will you do that?"

"Yes but . . ."

Ki stiffened as the dogs began to bark. He turned to follow their attention as Mike and Dennis came hurrying over to watch too.

"What is it?" Mike asked, rifle in hand. "There's still too much daylight for night raiders."

"It's a single horseman," Ki said, seeing a tall rider emerge out of the crimson sunset.

They were silent for a few minutes. Then Mike said, "It's trouble for me and that's for sure."

"Which is it?"

"It's Carrie's father, Tom Connors." Mike stepped out to meet the cattleman, saying, "That rifle in his fists isn't for decoration. Tom is not a man to waste words on small-talk."

"At least he isn't an ambusher," Sheila said.

Ki started to move forward, but Dennis stopped him with a shake of his head. "This is over the man's daughter," the Irish boy said. "I think it is best they settle it alone. Mike knew it had to happen sooner or later."

Ki held his place. He did not know this man but he did understand that, sooner or later, there was always a rivalry between a father and a suitor for a young woman's love. That was true in Japan and America, and while it usually did not involve the shedding of blood, often it did require just such an act.

The two men stopped at a distance of fifty feet apart. Tom Connors climbed down from his horse. He was big and solid, but Ki noticed that he dismounted with difficulty, and supposed that he suffered from an old injury of some kind.

"I came to kill you!" Connors yelled, "for ruining my daughter's reputation and my life."

"Your daughter is in love with me and I'm in love with her. Don't that count for anything?"

"I'd rather be dead than see her in love with a sheepman," Connors shouted.

"Then you'll get your wish," Mike bellowed.

Both men yanked their rifles to their shoulders, but Connors fired first. His bullet caught Mike in the thigh and spun him completely around. Mike grunted with pain when he hit the ground. He rolled, slammed the stock of his rifle to his shoulder, and fired in return. His bullet caught Tom Connors in the right shoulder and dropped him twisting into the dirt. The big cattleman gritted and managed to climb to his feet. Shoulder pumping blood, he tried to steady his aim, but when he pulled the trigger his shot went a mile wide. With a curse of frustration, he dropped the rifle and started to reach across his stomach to grab his holstered sixgun with his left hand.

Mike took aim and shot the sixgun right off his hip. The impact sent the big cattleman backward. He somehow managed to stand again. "Go ahead and kill me!" he raged, swaying on his feet. "You already have anyway by using my Carrie!"

Mike lowered his rifle. "I didn't 'use' her," he shouted in anger. "When you were in Cheyenne, we rode to Rock Springs and got married."

"You what?" Connors staggered backward as if he had been hit by another rifle slug.

"We got married, damn you!"

"Well, she didn't tell me that, either!"

"You two don't talk very well for a man who has only one daughter and a daughter that has only one father. Why don't you start?"

But the cattleman wasn't listening. "You got married? It's done?"

"That's right," Mike said through clenched teeth. He threw down his rifle, threw away his own sixgun, and hobbled forward with his fists clenched. "And if you say one more wrong word about her, I'm going to beat your goddamn head off!"

Big Tom Connors blinked into the fading sunset. He shook his head. Then he swore, "Well goddammit, if it's done, then it's done!"

He stuck out his hand. "I hate sheep, but I admire guts, which you have by the bucketful. Maybe we can even learn to be sociable with one another."

Mike stopped and studied the big outstretched hand. Finally, he reached for it. "We can if we each don't bleed to death jawin' here first."

Ki moved forward and grabbed Mike before the sheepman fell. He helped him over to the camp and cut his trouser leg with his *tanto* knife. A quick examination told him that Mike was lucky.

"The bullet missed the legbone," he said. "If it had shattered, you might have died of blood poisoning."

Mike smiled through clenched teeth. He looked over at big Tom Connors, who was sitting close by. Sheila had his shirt off and was already washing away the blood. "It's not too bad," she said. "Missed the lung, anyway. Dennis, we'll need some hot water. Heat up the fire."

"Could be dangerous," Mike grunted. "Maybe you had better let that go."

"Heat it up anyway," Ki ordered the young Irish shepherd. "It's no secret they know where we are. If they come, you'll have to stand and fight." Ki studied the sheepman's bloodied leg. "Mike, your running days are over."

They looked at Tom Connors. Of the two, his wound was the more serious. Ki went over to examine it after Sheila had washed away the dried blood. "As soon as the bleeding stops, I think we had better get you to a doctor," he said.

Connors nodded. As the campfire grew brighter it was easy to see that he was pale, but there was a faint smile that lifted the corners of his mouth. "Mike Bodie," he said, "now that you are married and in the family, I hope you and your father might show your good sense by selling off these damned bleating woolies and learn cowboyin'. Me and my boys will have you roping and branding steers in no time at all."

"You got that wrong for sure," Mike said. "This is sheep country. Anyone with half the sense God gave a goose could see that. Except for you and Ace Bard with all that irrigated pasture land along Skull Creek, the rest of this sagebrushy old country is made for browsing, not grazing."

Connors studied the fire for a minute. "You know, sometimes—and if you tell anyone I said this I'll take my gun to you again—sometimes, I almost think that a smart man would do well to have both cattle *and* a few sheep. That way, when the price at the stockyards falls off for one, maybe the other will carry the load."

"That makes sense, all right," Mike admitted grudgingly. "Even coming from a cattleman."

"I have to ask you this," Connors said. "What does my Carrie *really* think of your damned old woolies?"

Mike poked at the fire and sent sparks floating up into the air. "To be honest," he admitted sorrowfully, "she can't stand the sight or the smell of them."

Tom Connors grinned with relief. "I knew she wouldn't have gone completely daft."

He stood up to leave. "I think the bleeding has stopped," he said, and pushed out his big hand. "I guess you know I'd be lying if I said that I'm happy about the way this worked out. I ain't. But maybe some good will come of it, and if my Carrie loves you, then the rest don't matter."

Mike hobbled over to take the cattleman's hand. "I'll be good to her. Maybe we can work on that idea of yours about runnin' both sheep and cattle. I—"

He never finished. Out in the dark the muzzle blasts of rifles winked with death. The first slug blew Mike's hat off and creased him across the skull. The young sheepman dropped toward the fire, but Ki reacted so swiftly that he caught the man before he hit the flames. The samurai threw

162

himself and Mike into the brush as bullets began to rip through their camp. Dennis tried to race over to an old rifle, and took a bullet through the chest. He was dead before he struck the ground.

Tom Connors threw himself down and grabbed for his sixgun. Galway and Dublin growled. Then they disappeared into the brush as the flock began to scatter. The ambushers fired into their numbers, and the sheep cried pitifully and thrashed as they were hit on the run.

Ki heard a terrible growling and then a sharp, high, yipping sound.

"They're killing the dogs!" Tom Connors shouted in anger as he climbed to his feet and began to go after their attackers. "God damn them, I *like* dogs!"

But Ki was already far ahead of him. Once he was sure that Mike was still alive and that Sheila was down and out of sight, the samurai turned and darted into the brush. The image of that young Irish shepherd going down with a bullet through his chest filled Ki with a killing rage. He did not know how many ambushers Ace Bard had sent, and it did not matter. All that mattered was that a young man had just been brutally murdered, and the assassins were now killing more sheep and had probably shot at least one of the two remaining dogs.

"Wait for me!" Connor grunted.

But Ki wasn't about to wait. He ran swiftly, dodging through the tall brush, sometimes diving for cover and feeling the tops of bullet-riddled bushes flying across empty space where his head had just been. Ki followed the muzzle flashes. He heard one dog barking frantically and saw the flock of Bodie sheep running across the hills.

Then the samurai saw the three riflemen. They were

163

concealed behind some rocks, and were pouring a steady fire into both the camp and the fleeing band of sheep.

Ki angled sharply to his left. When the riflemen spotted him, he dove into the brush and began to crawl forward rapidly. He was now within twenty-five yards of the trio.

"Where the hell did he go?" Dade Cocker whispered urgently. "Did any of us hit him?"

"I think so," another answered without much conviction.

"Jesus Christ," Dade swore softly. "We got to kill them all. Come on, before they git away!"

They stood up cautiously and moved out of the rocks. Ki raised his head and saw them. The samurai's hand plucked two of his terrible *shuriken* star-blades from his vest. One in each hand, he came quickly to his feet.

"Look out!" one of the three yelled. "There he is!"

As their rifles swung in his direction like black, probing fingers of death, Ki hurled the *shuriken* blades. They gleamed momentarily in the moonlight, and then the first one stuck an assassin in the forehead. The man screamed and reached for his face. The sight so unnerved the second man that when another *shuriken* blade caught him in the throat, his lips were already distended in an expression of horror. He gurgled wetly, then staggered backward before falling to thrash in the brush.

Dade Cocker had a terrible premonition that his life was almost over. But as the samurai reached for his *tanto* blade, the Winchester Cattle Company gunman realized he had been spared. He raised his gun, took aim, and squeezed the trigger, certain that he could not miss.

But Tom Connors had already stopped. With his right shoulder carrying a bullet, he had used his left hand to hold his gun. He was not certain of his aim, but now, with the barrel of his Colt .45 laid solidly across his right forearm, he fired. The old Colt bucked, and Tom saw Dade Cocker crash over backward in the brush as Ki raised his hand to fling the deadly *tanto* blade.

"You would have been a shade too late, my friend," Tom said. "From now on, if there are more than two men that already have the drop on you, I'd advise you to get help first."

Ki shoved his blade back into its lacquered wooden sheath. "I'll try to remember that," he said, as he walked over to look at Dublin, who was lying wounded in the brush. The dog wimpered softly as Ki picked it up. Ki headed for the fire, saying a little prayer that the brave animal would live.

Chapter 15

From her hotel room in Skull Creek, Jessie watched the sun go down. She had a sense of foreboding. Things were moving very quickly, and tomorrow, she knew, all hell would break loose when the newspaper reporters and the governor's special assistant arrived in town. She had little doubt that Pete Bodie would be freed on bail and a new judge appointed to order a retrial in Cheyenne. There was just no way that anyone would acquit the Bodies, given the stranglehold the cattlemen had on Skull Creek.

Bill Lamar studied her closely. "Do you expect trouble tonight?"

Jessie nodded. "And—"

A knock at her door caused her to pause. Then she asked, "Who is it?"

"Ace Bard. I want to talk to you, Miss Starbuck."

Jessie glanced over at Bill. "Open the door and let's see if we can learn what the man has to say."

"Are you sure?"

"Of course. He isn't going to walk in here and attempt to murder us in this hotel room."

"Then why are you slipping that derringer into your skirt pocket?"

"Open the door," Jessie repeated.

When Ace stepped inside, he removed his white hat and gloves, then bowed formally. "You and I need to have a pleasant little conversation, Miss Starbuck. May I escort you to dinner?"

"I'm not hungry."

He looked at Bill and frowned. "I don't care for lawyers," he said, making it all the more clear by his expression. "Would you please ask the young man to leave us in private?"

"No."

Ace's pale cheeks flushed pink. "Very well. Then I'll get right to the point of my visit. I am prepared to have my prosecuting attorney, Mr. Jeters, cross-examine Mr. Melvin Dunn. Such a cross-examination might well turn up other . . . ah, shall we say, inconsistencies . . . in his testimony. Perjury is, of course, a criminal act and Mr. Dunn would face a short prison sentence. That being the case, the judge would have no choice but to rule that, contrary to what he had previously been led to believe, there is no real evidence against either Pete or Michael Bodie."

"Neat," Jessie said without enthusiasm. "So you pitch Melvin Dunn to the wolves and he goes to prison."

"He would be well compensated," Bard said sharply. "But that is of no concern to you."

"You're right. What does concern me is what your asking price might be."

"In return for dropped charges, I want the Bodies' promise that they will leave this valley forever, and deed me all their homesteaded ranchland."

"Why? Most of it is worthless for cattle. What importance is it to you?"

"I want to be the biggest rancher in western Wyoming, bar none," the man said. "I want to own more land than anyone in the Wind River valley. And besides, the Bodies do have some valuable water."

"I see." Jessie moved over to the window. "Why are you telling me this? Why not walk over to the jail and ask Pete Bodie if he's interested? After all, it is *his* land and *his* life we are discussing."

"I already talked to him late this afternoon. He said 'hell no.'"

"Then I echo that sentiment."

Ace took a threatening step forward. Outwardly, he appeared cool and collected, but now, as Jessie gazed into those stone-dead eyes of his, she saw the fires of hell burning hotly from the depths of his dark soul. Jessie's hand moved to her derringer. She saw Bill's hand stray toward the gun he had taken to wearing.

But Ace caught himself and bridled his temper. "I talked to the telegraph operator. He told me, with some reluctance, that you have sent for quite a collection of newspaper reporters, as well as the governor himself."

Jessie said nothing. It was not important that, at the very last moment, the governor had been forced to send a representative on his behalf.

"So," Ace said heavily. "Because the stage that Pete Bodie will take to prison does not leave Skull Creek until late tomorrow afternoon, you probably feel very secure that you have beaten the cattlemen in this valley."

"I never feel overconfident of anything," Jessie told the

man. "I've learned from my father and from hard experience to know otherwise."

"You're as intelligent as you are lovely," Ace said. He turned to Bill Lamar. "As I said, I don't like lawyers, though I admit they sometimes prove necessary. You, young man, show promise, while Mr. Jeter shows signs of mental decay. Should you like to work for me in the future, you may write."

"Not a snowball's chance in hell."

A small place to the left of Ace Bard's eye twitched. He whirled and left them, slamming the door in his wake.

"He's furious," Jessie said. "Mad enough and desperate enough to kill."

"I shouldn't have been so blunt."

"It wouldn't have made any difference." Jessie stared out her window. "His back is to the wall and he knows it. He *has* to kill the Bodies now. And you know what I think?"

"What?"

"I think he knew it from the very beginning. Only now, he has just tonight."

"That means he could have men hitting the Bodies' camp right now."

"Yes. But with Ki and Michael out there, I feel sure they can handle things. Our job is to protect Pete from being murdered."

"How?"

Jessie began to pace back and forth. "Let me think on it for a few minutes. But whatever we do, we have to act fast. It's dusk, and even if I hadn't realized it before Ace visited us, I know now that time is running out on our friend the sheepherder."

• • •

Jessie watched as Bill staggered along the boardwalk with an empty whiskey bottle in his fist. He was singing a surprisingly bawdy song and shouting at the top of his lungs. To all appearances, he was dead drunk on his feet.

A prostitute with half of her bosom falling out of a low-cut satin dress called to him from the second-story window of the other hotel in town. "Hey, sweetie, why don't you come on up here and I'll really show you a good time!"

Bill staggered to a halt, grabbed a porch post to support himself, and twirled slowly around. With a loose grin on his face, he looked up at her. It appeared as if he was having difficulty in focusing his eyes. "Hey, honey," he called, "as soon as I free my client from this goddamn jail I'll just do that!"

"Awww. Let old Pete sleep tonight," the whore called, throwing him kisses and leaning out so far it looked as if she were completely top-heavy. "We got some lovin' to do!"

Jessie frowned. *Come on Bill,* she thought with mounting irritation. *Don't be so distracted by that shameless floozy!*

"Be back in a while!" Bill called drunkenly. "What's your name?"

"Ruby Dooh!" she yodeled as several other men whistled.

One pulled money out of his pocket, counted it quickly, and yelled, "How much for a quickie, Ruby?"

"Two dollars, honey! Five dollars will get you an hour in paradise and ten will kill you with pleasure!"

"I ain't ready for death or paradise," the man called up

to her as he hurried towards the hotel. "But I sure could use a quickie!"

Ruby laughed, and the coarse sound bounced up and down the narrow corridor of businesses. "See you right after this one!" she called to Bill Lamar.

"Okay!" he yelled, turning his face to the black night sky before stumbling on toward the sheriff's office. "Whoowee, Ruby Dooh!"

Jessie shook her head. Either that boy showed promise as a fine actor, or else he had some devilishness in his heart. She watched him come to a swaying standstill before the sheriff's office. Several cowboys had also come out to watch as Bill used his empty whiskey bottle to slam against the door. He was so exuberant that the bottle shattered before Sheriff Pettit could get the door opened.

Jessie could see them clearly. The sheriff's sheer bulk dwarfed the young attorney, but Bill stood his ground. They argued, their words indistinct until the sheriff suddenly roared, "That ties it, goddammit! You're under arrest for being drunk and disorderly!"

And then the sheriff grabbed Bill, yanked him completely off his feet, and hurled him into the office. The door slammed. Cowboys in the street roared with laughter and Ruby Dooh called invitingly, "It appears my evenin' of pleasure is open once again to you boys! Which one of you has a strong enough heart to stand the pleasures I await to unfold?"

Jessie watched them pool their money and slap it down on the boardwalk before they began to cut a deck of cards for the winner.

Bill Lamar hit the cell hard. Still pretending to be drunk, he turned to see the lawman's face, which had become ugly with meanness. The man said, "Goddamn, but I'm glad to have you here like this. I been a-watchin' you in that court-room and a-wantin' to smash your smart-alecky face down your throat. Now, I do believe I will."

"Leave him alone!" Pete Bodie yelled, coming off his mattress and grabbing the cell bars. "I swear I'll tell on you if you hurt this boy."

The sheriff just laughed with derision. "Pete, you're gonna be dead before midnight anyway, so shut up and let me to my fun."

"Run, boy!" the old sheepman yelled frantically. "He's about to tear your drunken head clean off!"

Bill grinned stupidly. But he stepped forward, and when the sheriff swung at him, he drove the toe of his polished shoe right up between the big man's legs and crushed his testicles.

Sheriff Leon T. Pettit's eyes rolled up in his head. His lips formed a distended circle and he went white-faced. As a howl filled the sheriff's throat, Bill whipped out his six-gun and brought it down hard across Sheriff Pettit's naked forehead.

The sheriff went down so hard he seemed to bounce on the floor.

Bill holstered his gun and said to the amazed prisoner, "This being a lawyer sure isn't anything like I was told it'd be by my uncle."

"Jesus Christ!" Pete breathed. "You ain't drunk at all!"

"Nope. And we have to get you out of this jail before whoever is coming to finish you off shows up to do the job. Where are the keys?"

Pete gestured over to the wall. "Usually, they're hung on that peg over there. But not tonight. That's mighty strange."

"I guess I'll have to search him," Bill said unhappily. "I was hoping to avoid it."

"Well, hurry up if there really is someone coming to blow a hole in my hull!"

Bill searched frantically. "No keys."

"Damn!" Pete groused. "Check his desk."

Bill checked out the man's desk. "Not in here either."

"Well, what could have happened to them? A sheriff has got to have the keys to his own jail cell."

Bill took a deep breath and exhaled slowly to calm himself. "I'm afraid I can guess where those keys are," he said finally.

"Where?"

"Whoever is coming to kill you has got them."

Pete swallowed nervously. "You had better give me a gun," he said.

Bill relieved the sheriff of his sidearm, then dragged the heavy lawman out of sight behind his desk.

"What you going to do now?"

Bill crouched down behind the desk. "I guess I'll just wait until whoever comes to kill you shows up. Then I'll try to kill him first."

"Good boy! After this night, you might just decide to chuck the lawyerin' business and become a hired gunman!"

Bill ignored the sheepman's cackling laughter.

When the door opened, it opened fast. Bill and Pete both were half asleep when three men came bursting inside with drawn guns.

Pete did not ask them if they wanted to raise their hands in surrender, as Bill was prepared to do. Instead, the old man just opened fire. One of the gunmen yelped with pain, and the other two exchanged bullets as Bill jumped up and caught them in a crossfire.

A gunman went down, and the other two would have bolted and run except that Bill shouted, "Freeze or you'll never get through that door alive!"

They froze. His hand was shaking so bad that the gun barrel was jumping all over the place. But the young attorney managed to say, "Hand over the cell keys and be quick about it!"

"He's got 'em!" one said, pointing to the man on the floor.

Bill found the keys, but while distracted, the other two shot out the door and escaped.

"Let them go!" Pete called. "And get me outta here before the whole durned town comes runnin'!"

Bill did just that. In a moment, they were running out, taking a quick left into the alley and making good their escape.

They didn't have far to run. Jessie was now in the alley, and three horses were ready and waiting.

"It's one o'clock in the morning. What happened in there that took so long?"

"Couldn't find the damned keys!" Bill shouted as they galloped down the alley.

Jessie held her silence. She could find out the details later. But for right now, things were going according to plan. They would find the Bodie flock and join forces. By tomorrow at noon, the newspaper reporters and the governor's assistant would be in Skull Creek.

But until then, they would stand against the cattlemen alone and to the very end.

Chapter 16

Jessie could see the first gray fingers of dawn on the eastern horizon. One by one the stars died, and she looked up to see an owl glide silently across a sky that was even now beginning to be touched with the salmon and golden colors of daybreak.

Behind them, penned by rocks and scrub timber, the Bodie flock was just beginning to awaken. Lambs bleated softly to be fed by their mothers. Ewes bleated in return as they stiffly climbed to their feet and searched for browse.

"It's going to be a beautiful day if we live through it," Sheila Abraham decided out loud as she waited nearby with a pistol clenched in her fist.

Beside her, Bill said, "We'll live. Ace Bard can't have *that* many gunmen."

"Don't bet on it," Mike said tensely. "Besides, it isn't just Bard that will be coming; it will be every damned cattleman in the valley."

"Except Tom Connors," Ki corrected. "If I am any judge of character, he would side with us before the cattlemen."

"I wish I could believe that," Mike said. "Sure, we

shook hands and he allowed I was his new son-in-law, but he's almost *got* to stand with the other cattlemen."

"That's right," old Pete said. "Them cattlemen hate sheep worse than ticks, and we're the last flock in this valley. If we live, other sheepmen might come back and the range wars will start up all over again. Tom Connors knows that. He'll line up with Ace and the rest of them murderin' cow lovers."

Ki was not convinced. "I think you badly underestimated the man."

"I hope so." Despite those words, Mike Bodie did not sound confident.

The samurai, always the one most alert to danger, said, "I think I heard the sound of a shod horse's hoof striking a rock. Listen!"

Jessie had been only half listening to the whispered conversation of her friends. But now, Galway's throat filled with a growl and Dublin, though grievously wounded, echoed that warning.

"They're coming in now," Jessie said, her eyes straining into the growing daylight. "They will probably come at us from all sides."

Jessie was right. Rifle fire suddenly opened up and hot lead came flying in from all directions. Jessie and the others ducked into the rocks as bullets whined off granite and then ricocheted meanly. A stray bullet pricked Jessie's forearm. Another kicked splinters of rock into Bill's eyes, almost blinding him. Before another bullet could take his life, Sheila pushed him down, no doubt saving him.

"Everyone stay down!" Jessie cried as they flattened among the rocks.

"There must be fifty men out there!" Mike growled. "They got us pinned down good."

Even Ki had to agree. The samurai was using a gun now, and wondering if they could possibly hold out until darkness, when he would be able to go out among them.

"Everyone save your ammunition in case they are foolish enough to charge us," Jessie said.

"They won't." Ki looked out between the rock and instantly a hail of bullets screamed in and bit into the rock.

"What do we do now?" Sheila asked quietly.

"We wait," Jessie answered. "We have food and water; there is nothing they can do to us unless they want to pay the price of a charge, which would cost too many of their numbers. Time is on our side."

Waiting, however, proved difficult. The morning passed with sporadic gunfire and it soon became evident that Ace Bard and his gunmen and friends were attempting to ricochet their bullets around in the nest of rocks and either blind someone as they had nearly done to Bill, or else hit them with a stray bullet.

Jessie and Ki watched the sun inch upward and finally begin its long and terribly slow decline toward the western horizon. No one talked much, and whenever bullets caromed off the rocks they all hugged the ground and tensed their bodies, waiting for a fatal hit.

Ki took his place beside Jessie. "I don't think they can afford to take too much more time at this," he said. "Time *is* on our side. Those newspaper reporters and the governor's representative must be in Skull Creek by now, and they're going to be asking a lot of tough questions."

"I know," Jessie replied. "Like, what happened to us?"

"That's right."

Jessie managed a thin smile. "They'll have the answer quick enough. I left a letter for all of them at the telegraph operator's office."

"You did?"

"Yes—while waiting for Bill and Pete to make good their jailbreak. It occurred to me that we had better tell them exactly what was going on. Of course, I didn't know precisely where you and the flock were, but I had a general idea."

"Do you think the telegraph operator will give them the letter?"

"I paid him a hundred dollars last night, and promised him another hundred when we returned. That's at least six months' income. He'll pass along the letter all right. But those people aren't going to stand up to Ace Bard's small army."

"At least they'll know the truth if we are overrun and killed," Ki said.

"That's not much consolation, but it *is* some."

Another rifle shot was instantly followed by the terrible cry of a wounded sheep. Galway growled deep in his throat and the hair on his back lifted threateningly. The dog came swiftly to his feet and would have jumped out of their cover of rocks and raced to his flock, but Mike caught the animal and held it down.

"Stay!" he ordered.

Galway whined as another shot rang out and a second ewe was dropped to thrash in the sagebrush.

"Goddamn them!" Mike shouted after looking over the rocks. "They're not even trying to kill my sheep outright! They want them to *suffer!*"

Ki knew that to be the truth. All through ancient history, armies had used the same technique to break down the resistance of their foes. To capture a spy and torture him slowly outside the walls of a city or a fort was an old and very effective weapon, almost guaranteed to undermine the will of the defenders.

More rifles opened up and Jessie heard the sound of bullets ripping into the flock. The isolated bleats became a chorus of death. Jessie wanted nothing more than to cover her ears and drown the hideous sound.

Mike gripped his rifle and started to come to his feet.

"No!" his father shouted. "They're just sheep, boy!"

But Mike was already rising. Ki had anticipated this, and even before the young sheepman's head lifted above the rocks, the samurai's fingers were reaching out to cramp a vital pressure point. Mike struggled but a moment; then he collapsed.

There were tears in Pete's rheumy old eyes when he said, "Thanks for saving his life. I almost wish you'd do the same to me. I'm not sure how long I can stand hearing them slaughter our flock. Those sheep are like . . . like children to us."

"I know," Ki said. "But—"

Whatever he was about to say was forgotten as a large body of horsemen suddenly appeared on the horizon. They were coming on the run, the trail of their dust rooster-tailing high into the fading light of day.

"Who is it?" Jessie asked, turning to the samurai, who had the keenest eyesight of any man she had ever known.

Ki lifted his head quickly, but was greeted by a swarm of bullets. He dropped back down behind the rocks and said, "I can't tell yet."

But the staccato rattle of distant gunfire told Jessie it was help, and it was coming fast. She lifted her head a moment later and was gratified to see that Ace Bard and his men had swung around and opened fire on the attacking force of riders.

"Let's go!" Jessie cried, leaping out of the rocks and sprinting forward with her gun bucking in her fist.

The samurai was right beside her. Bill Lamar, his tear-filled eyes finally clearing, came stumbling out along with the old shepherd.

It was a rout. Big Tom Connors, his shoulder swathed in a bandage, shooting left-handed, wasn't hitting anything, but his cowboys along with the U.S. marshal the governor had sent were doing just fine.

Ace Bard, so evident in that big white Stetson and his gloves, stood and shouted, "Hold your ground!"

But his men were falling, and others began to race for their horses. Ace swore and turned to his own horse.

Ki was still twenty feet away when the cattle baron reined his mount around hard and started to drive his spurs into the animal's flanks. Ki reached inside his vest for his last *shuriken* blade.

"No!" Jessie cried, "I want him alive."

The samurai quickly unloosed from his narrow waist the *surushin* rope with its leather-covered balls of steel. Faster than the eye could see, he had the rope whirling twice overhead and then flying out. Ace's horse was carrying him away, but not fast enough. The *surushin* wrapped itself around his upper body, binding his arms to his side. The man's reins fell and the horse plunged on, totally out of control.

Jessie was in the saddle and racing after the cattleman. This was much too rough a country to race a horse across blindly. There were rocks and holes, hidden arroyos choked with brush and . . .

"Ahhhh!"

She heard Ace scream as his horse somersaulted and completely disappeared, as if swallowed up by the very earth itself. But a split second later, the horse leaped out of the ground and went racing away as if the very devil were tied to its tail. Jessie heard Ace scream again and again, and then his voice went silent. She reined in hard, sending her own mount to a sliding stop that ended right before a deep pit that was roiling with poisonous snakes.

Jessie recoiled in shock and revulsion, and her horse whirled in terror. Jessie dismounted and let the crazed animal gallop away as she approached the pit and watched the deadly vipers. She swallowed dryly as she saw rattlers as thick around as her forearm crawling all over the body of the dying cattleman. Mercifully, their venom and the terrible fall had already caused Ace to lose consciousness. It was a sight that Jessie would not soon forget, though she would certainly try.

Another big rattler struck Bard in the side and his body convulsed, then twitched spasmodically. The gun in Jessie's fist sent a bullet exploding through the viper's triangle-shaped little head. The other snakes buzzed even more ominously. There had to be at least thirty of them.

Jessie shook her head as if she could forever dispel the sight she now beheld. This was not the first rattlesnake pit she had ever seen, but it was the only one that she had ever seen a man die in.

She walked away quickly, concentrating on the sunset and the smell of the sage—anything to rid her of what she had just witnessed.

When Tom Connors came loping over and offered to give her a ride back to camp, Jessie gratefully accepted.

"What happened to Ace?" he asked.

Jessie told him in as few words as possible. The cattleman muttered, "Worst death I ever heard of."

"It's over."

"I'm ashamed of myself and the cowboys that kilt all those sheep. My own boys are ashamed too."

"It's done. Why don't you and Mike try to be friends? He's a damned good man. You saw that when he stood up to you. Mr. Connors, you could have done a whole lot worse."

"I know that now. I mean to mend my fences—sort of make sure that something like this never happens again in these parts. The killin' is over."

Jessie nodded. When she reached camp, she had to explain what happened to Ace again, and their reaction was the same as hers had been.

Carrie was cradling Mike in her arms. Sheila Abraham was standing close to Bill Lamar. When Jessie came up to them, she said, "How are your eyes?"

"They'll be all right," the attorney replied.

"We'll be leaving Wyoming on the first train."

Jessie looked at Sheila. "At the bank in Skull Creek you have a significant amount of money in account."

"I do?" Sheila did not understand.

"It's yours for saving both Mike and Ki that night. It was a brave act."

"I can't take money for that."

Jessie just shrugged. "You lost everything, including your husband. Maybe with the money I've left, you might want to use some of it to go to Boston and see that plastic surgeon."

Unbidden, Sheila's hand reached up to touch the disfiguring scar on her cheek. "Do you really think he could . . ."

"Yes," Jessie said with emphasis. "He definitely can, and after I return to Circle Star, he'll be expecting your visit."

Sheila threw her arms around Jessie and cried until Bill gently pried her loose. "Miss Starbuck," he said, "before you send me off somewhere to learn your business, I'd like to take a month or two off."

He toed the ground self-consciously. "I know it seems wrong, my asking for time away before I've even really started working for your company, but I think I'd like to accompany Sheila to Boston. She shouldn't be alone in a big city."

Jessie suppressed a knowing smile. She had seen this coming. There was a strong physical attraction between these two. "That sounds like a fine idea, Bill. The job will be waiting whenever you both visit us in Texas."

They blushed.

"Miss Starbuck?"

Jessie turned to the man who had spoken her name. "Yes?"

"I was sent here by the governor. Name is David Waters and this here is Marshal Trump."

The marshal nodded. "Me and my deputies have been sent by the governor to clean up Skull Creek and put an end to the trouble. I'm also authorized to conduct a hearing on the murder of Elvin Pattison. But," he added quickly, "that's just a formality. From what your letter said and from the testimony I'm sure we'll get from those we apprehend, the Bodies will be completely exonerated."

"What about the judge?"

"Disbarment," Waters said grimly. "I happen to also be the president of the Wyoming Bar Association and the evidence is overwhelming against the man. He might even face criminal charges."

Jessie nodded. "Then that about ties it up."

* * *

And it did. Two days later she, Ki, Bill, and Sheila were at
Rock Springs, waiting for the Union Pacific to carry them
away. As they were standing on the railroad platform, Jessie turned to Tom Connors, who had personally driven
them over in his wagon. "What about the body of Ace
Bard?" she asked.

"We decided to leave him and the other snakes right
where they was. The boys and I filled that pit with rocks.
We wanted to make damn sure that no other poor fool rode
into it by mistake."

Jessie said, "I hope you keep your promise about running a few sheep on your range. You set the example in
that valley, Tom. And don't Mike and your daughter make
a fine couple?"

"I reckon I seen worse," the cattleman acknowledged.

"Why don't you take them out to dinner and order lamb
chops, so that Mike will know that you meant what you
said the other night about sheep?"

But Connor shook his head gravely. "I might raise a few
of them damn woolies to keep peace in this valley, but I
danged sure ain't about to poison myself by eatin' them!"

Jessie nodded her head in agreement and whispered,
"Don't tell anybody, but as a cattle rancher, I feel exactly
the same way."